Stonewall Inn Mysteries
Michael Denneny, General Editor

BY MARK RICHARD ZUBRO

The "Tom and Scott" Mysteries

A Simple Suburban Murder
Why Isn't Becky Twitchell Dead?
The Only Good Priest
The Principal Cause of Death

The "Paul Turner" Mysteries

Sorry Now?

The Principal Cause of Death

Mark Richard Zubro

St. Martin's Press
New York

Library of Congress Cataloging-in-Publication Data

Zubro, Mark Richard
      The principal cause of death / Mark Richard Zubro.
          p.   cm.
      ISBN 0-312-07767-X (hc)
      ISBN 0-312-09896-0 (pbk.)
      I. Title.
      PS3576.U225P75   1992
      813'.54—dc20   92-1100
                                  CIP

First Edition: May 1992
First Paperback Edition: October 1993

10 9 8 7 6 5 4 3 2 1

For Michael and learning
the meaning of friendship

Acknowledgments

For their invaluable assistance I wish to thank Mike Kushner, Peg Panzer, Rick Paul, and Kathy Pakieser-Reed.

The
Principal
Cause
of
Death

1

Outside my classroom windows, red and gold autumn leaves danced and swayed against the backdrop of magically clear blue skies. Even the aged panes, unwashed by countless janitors, couldn't keep out the glory of the afternoon. Water seeped around the warped and sagging sashes whenever it rained. After each blast of a storm, I expected to find glass strewn across the floor, but over the years they'd held. The day outside sparkled through them.

Fifth period, lunch just over, the quiet murmurs of education drifted through the hallways of Grover Cleveland High School. I leaned over Dennis Olsen's desk, for the fifteenth attempt since school began to convince him that capital letters did indeed come at the beginning of every sentence. I dipped deep into my reservoir of teacher patience and began to explain again.

This was Life Skills English class, which means, Make sure they can sign their name and count their change but don't expect much more. I had higher expectations. I wanted them to be able to read and fill out forms, balance a checkbook, and perhaps acquire another skill or two. I knew I couldn't turn them into nuclear scientists, but I wanted more than bare literacy.

Dan Bluefield banged open the classroom door, pushed his way down the aisle toward me, and thrust his pass in my direction. "Here, Mr. Mason," he said.

An inch before my fingers touched it, he let the piece of paper drop to the floor. He turned on his heel, shoved a kid out of a desk, and sat down.

Grover Cleveland High School has had problem kids over the years, and eventually I got most of them in this class.

Dan Bluefield was the toughest kid I'd tried to teach since Dennis Rogers fourteen years ago. Among Dennis's many achievements at Grover Cleveland: biting off the tip of a kid's finger; attempting to set fire to the gym; and attacking and wounding three teachers. Dennis earned straight F's in my class, managing to be disruptive, abusive, and rude. He'd made my days a living hell. I sighed with relief every time I saw his name on the absence list. I cheered for joy whenever they announced an assembly during the period I was supposed to have him in class. Last I heard, he was serving eight to ten years for armed robbery somewhere in Texas.

Dan Bluefield made Dennis look like an angelic first-grader. Parents, teachers, police, and a variety of state agencies had been trying to cope with him for years.

To his dubious credit, Steve Bailey, the kid who Dan shoved out of the chair, tried to punch back. Dan was six feet tall, thin, and wiry. Steve only came up to his shoulder. Without standing up, Dan gave Steve a powerful shove. Steve tumbled over several desks and fell to his knees. I got between them and restrained an enraged Steve.

"Dean's office," I said to Dan.

"Just came from there," he sneered.

At that moment I hated him more than anything in the universe. Hassling me was one thing; hurting other kids in my class was not going to happen as long as I was able to stop it. If I had wizard's powers, I'd have fried Dan on the spot. I wanted to take his sneers, smirks, and stupidity and beat the living shit out of him, but eighteen years of patience and training won out, and I said, "Dan, you have to go to the dean's office. You know you can't assault students."

2

He smirked, "I didn't assault him. He was in the way. I just asked him to move."

The other kids in the class watched the confrontation. For them this was great entertainment. No matter what happened, I knew they'd be on Dan's side. Didn't make any difference who was right or how many times Dan had made them miserable. One of the verities of the teaching world is that the students will take the kid's side versus the teacher. You cannot win a confrontation with kids. You can flatter your ego that you got the best of them, but you can't beat them.

The snotty little creep still sat in the desk he'd evicted Steve from. With both hands I grabbed the top of the desk. My knuckles turned white and I felt the desktop wobble. The desks were forty years old and years of seating teenagers made them treacherous at times. Last year one had collapsed under the minuscule weight of a scrawny freshman.

With my face an inch from his, I said, "Get out. Now. I, for one, am sick to death of putting up with you."

He laughed at me. He knew I wouldn't hit him. All the rules forbade hitting students, and ninety nine point nine percent of the time, I agreed with those rules.

I put more pressure on the old wooden desktop. It gave a groan and snapped in two. Dan jumped up and eyed me warily, edging toward the door. Grasping a piece of desk top in each hand, I advanced toward him. Dan snarled and spat, sent another kid and desk sprawling, and stormed toward the exit. His parting shot just before he slammed the door was "Fuck you, faggot."

I strode to the intercom and called the office to let them know they had to be on the lookout for Dan.

Very little education got done for the fifteen minutes left in the period. I'd surprised myself with the towering anger I'd felt and how much I'd wanted to hurt the kid.

Class ended, the kids left, and I sat at my desk, staring out the window. I watched the breeze play with the undropped leaves as dappled sunlight created shifting patterns on desktops, chalkboard, and floor. In two weeks Scott and I would be among the glorious fall colors in the woods in our cabin on Lake Superior. I gazed at a group of kids, dressed for PE class, trotting under the trees on their way to the athletic fields beyond.

The perfect weather couldn't prevent me from getting angrier and more frustrated. Fifteen minutes of planning-period time passed before I gave up trying to get any work done. I walked down the ancient and worn halls to the library. Small knots of students worked silently at the tables. I found Meg Swarthmore, the librarian, at the front desk.

"What's wrong, Tom?" she said as soon as she saw me.

I motioned her into the office behind the desk. We could talk in privacy, but she could still keep an eye on her charges through the glass in the door.

At sixty-six Meg is semiretired, working flexible hours, setting her own schedule. She used to be the ultimate clearinghouse for all school gossip, but she's given that up as well. "Too many hassles with the younger teachers" is the way she put it to me. She's a tiny woman, not much over five feet tall, and plump in a grandmotherly way.

I told her what just happened, including how badly I wanted to hurt Bluefield.

"You're human," she said. "You've done wonders with some of these kids in the past. You will in the future. Why should you be immune from wanting to flatten the little creep into tiny pieces? Every teacher he's had since the first grade has wanted to do the same." She told me about an episode when Dan was in the fifth grade. Meg'd been working for a few days in the elementary-school library, filling in for a sick coworker.

"Bluefield tried to glue a stack of books together. I told him to stop. He wouldn't. When I reached to take the books away from him, he tried to slap me. I was too quick for him. I held his arm, and when he couldn't get away, he tried to throw a fit. You know how sympathetic I am to that kind of nonsense."

4

Meg was tough. I'd seen her cow the 250-pound starting center on the football team. She never touched the kid, but she backed him up against his locker and let him have it, all in a calm near-whisper. The boy was in tears before she let him go.

She sighed. "Must have been seven years ago that I had my run-in with him. I almost got in trouble for restraining the little monster."

"You never told me," I said.

She mused a minute. "I thought I did. It was the usual nonsense. The father got all bent out of shape. Claimed I was picking on his creepy offspring. He tried to accuse me of inflicting corporal punishment."

In the State of Illinois teachers have the right to use corporal punishment on children. Different school districts have varying policies on using the right. In some places only the principal can administer corporal punishment. In the River's Edge school system, however, it is strictly forbidden for anyone to hit a kid.

Meg said, "You remember the administrator we had at the time? What's his name—Wellington? Napoleon? Whatever. He had this big investigation. Several fifth graders claimed I attacked Bluefield. The principal called parents trying to get them to twist more information out of the students. It was almost as if he were trying to build up a case against me. He even had several meetings with the parents of the students. Totally nuts. The only thing that saved me was that a couple of the kids who gave the strongest testimony about my alleged attack hadn't even been in the library at the time. One had even been absent from school that day. I only found that out because one of the parents thought the whole investigation was silly nonsense and called to tell me. I found out from her that her kid hadn't been in school that day. It blew over after a week or so, although they still put a nasty letter about the incident in my file, as if I really cared about that."

A few administrators use the teachers' personnel files to get revenge. They can lie on evaluation forms or write letters that are totally false, and put them into a teacher's file. Essentially a teacher can't do a thing about it. The teacher can write a rebuttal and have it attached to the record, but any stranger reading the file is at least going to have some question about what happened. The most difficult, but probably the best, attitude for most teachers to take is that this is an administrator's petty way of exacting childish revenge and to forget about it. The truth is no one outside the school district can see what's in your file, anyway.

We talked until the bell rang for last hour. Still a little annoyed, I went through the motions of a Seniors Honors English class. Eventually the machinations of Richard II, and explaining them to high-school kids, began to absorb my attention. For the moment I forgot about Bluefield.

At the end of class Georgette Constantine, the school secretary, showed up at my door with a note telling me to meet with Robert Jones, the principal, at four-thirty about the incident with Dan Bluefield.

I had tickets for that night to see Scott pitch in the last game of the season. I didn't want to be late. I asked Georgette if I could see Jones any earlier. She said he had meetings until then.

I sat down to grade papers while I waited. Kurt Campbell, our union president and one of my best friends on the staff, stopped by as he was leaving. I told him about the incident with Bluefield. He told me I didn't have anything to worry about in terms of the contract or the legality of what happened and not to worry about it.

Around four I strolled down to the teachers' lounge to get a can of soda and relax for a few minutes.

Outside the science lab I heard the tinkling of broken glass. I glanced up and down the deserted corridor. Lockers with paint chipping from years of use, lights in the ceiling with fixtures worn and cracked, and a tile floor gray from thousands of trampling kids and scrubbing custodians. All this, but nary a human. Sunshine streamed from a few of the windows in the doors of rooms that faced west.

The tinkling came again. I walked to the door of the science lab. Since the lab was on the east side of the building, little light filtered into the room. As I reached for the doorknob, I heard a resounding crash from inside. I hesitated: Should I go for help or barge in?

Suddenly I had no decision to make. The door to the room crashed open. Dan Bluefield stood in front of me. He squawked and backed into the room. I followed. The front of the room was totally intact. But glass-fronted floor-to-ceiling cabinets stretched the entire length of the rear wall of the room, and shards of glass from one of the doors covered three feet of floor in front of it. Upended microscopes and shattered beakers obscured the top of the nearest table.

Then I noticed her, cowering in a corner. A woman in her early twenties, with blood dripping from her nose and a cut on her lip. I recognized her as one of the student teachers from Lincoln University.

"He hit me!" she wailed.

I moved to go to her. When Bluefield tried to block my way, he took his eyes off her, and she darted toward the door and fled down the hall. I hoped she would send help; because I'd moved to help the woman, Bluefield was between me and the door.

"Why, Dan?" I asked.

A switchblade appeared in his hand.

I backed away from him, my eyes frantically searching for the intercom button. I'd been in the Marines in Vietnam, but I wasn't eager to risk nearly twenty-year-old skills against his youth—and a weapon. I might have tried shoving him aside and dashing down the hall for help, but the expert way he held his knife, and his aggressive stance, made it doubtful that such a strategy would succeed.

In the dim light his gray eyes appeared almost translucent. "You want to talk about this, Dan?" I asked.

His response was to begin edging steadily toward me. I spotted the intercom switch in the wall near the exit, under the American flag.

He saw my eyes flicker toward it. He gave a short laugh. "No help coming for you, faggot teacher. I'm going to hurt you a little bit."

"Easy, Dan," I said. "Do you really want to do this?"

"Oh, I really do, Mr. Mason. I really, truly do. I want to hurt you real bad."

"Come on, Dan, give me the knife."

"No way. Not until I'm done." He made a pass in my direction with the weapon.

I moved so that one of the science tables stood between us. I hoped another late-staying teacher might pass the door, making for the lounge, as I had been. Perhaps even some of the kids staying late for clubs or sports who might have a locker at this end of the building. So far I heard nothing.

Dan advanced slowly, keeping himself between me and the door. He tried a brief lunge across the top of a table. It squeaked loudly as the weight of his body shoved it into me. The table's motion startled him and for a moment he tottered and stumbled. I grabbed for the arm with the knife and missed. The table swung again, unbalancing me. He lunged forward. I twisted, dropped to the floor, and felt, more than saw, the knife whish past my ear. I scrambled under a table. He flipped it over. I stood quickly and he came at me. I tried to dodge the knife and tripped over a table leg. As I fell, I saw the knife come slashing down. I threw my right arm up to ward off the blow. The knife tore through my sport jacket and several inches of me. I howled in pain and yanked my arm away. His thrust and my movement unbalanced him, and he fell.

Blind fury and aching pain took over. I was on him in an instant. His youth and energy allowed him to get to his feet, but seconds later I had the hand with the knife in a viselike grip. I heard a snap, the knife dropped, and he bellowed in pain. I didn't stop. Years of training and patience were gone in that instant. I wanted to hurt him, for every taunt, rude remark, stupid smirk, and asshole comment. My fist slamming into his midsection took most of the fight out of him. A punch to the kidneys straightened him up. A knee to the groin doubled him back over. I shoved him as hard as I could. He tumbled backwards, slammed into the wall, then, slowing, slid down, coming to rest on his fucked-up teenaged ass.

I heard a rustle in the doorway. Two kids I didn't know stood there, mouths agape, staring at the destruction. "Get help," I ordered.

They disappeared.

I reached the intercom and punched the button for the office. Georgette Constantine came on. Suddenly I realized I was breathing heavily and could barely speak.

"Send help, Georgette," I gasped, "to the science lab."

She recognized my voice. "Mr. Mason, Tom, are you all right?"

"Just hurry, Georgette."

I tore off my suit coat and examined my arm. The cut stretched for four inches about halfway between my elbow and wrist. It hurt like hell, but didn't bleed as much as I expected. Mustn't have hit a vein or artery. I felt woozy for a moment, and instinctively reached out for support. When my right arm hit the wall, I cried out in pain. For an instant, looking at the cut, I saw it went deep, to the bone.

I slumped into the teacher's chair to wait for help to arrive. Dan lay against the wall moaning, using his left hand alternately to try to ease his right wrist, clutch at his midsection, or cup his crotch.

"You busted my wrist, you bastard!"

I felt my anger subside and found guilt and remorse setting in. And then I was angry at myself anew for the last two feelings. The kid had attacked me. What was I supposed to do?

Minutes later janitors, administrators, teachers, and police filled the room. They took Dan off to the hospital. Meg drove me to the emergency room of River's Edge Community Medical Center. After the administration of antiseptic, stitches, bandages, and pain pills, we left the hospital.

She drove me back to school. I needed my briefcase

from my room. I also wanted to talk to any cops who might still be around.

In the school office Georgette saw me and quickly came over to offer help and kind words. She clucked at the bandages and told me she could drive me home if necessary. I still wanted to get to the baseball game. It was already six, and I felt okay enough to drive. I told her no thanks.

But Jones came to the door of his office. "I want to talk to you. Now, Mr. Mason."

He radiated anger as he seated himself behind his desk in his oversized chair. The most unusual thing about his office was that a bookcase and part of one wall were dedicated to polar bears. Cuddly white stuffed animals in all sizes filled the bookshelves. The pictures on the walls emphasized the mother bears with their cubs. The rest of the office contained a computer terminal, a fake-wood desk, brown-cloth-covered chairs, and a mustard-colored rug with flecks of gold throughout. The window in the wall behind him looked out on the changing leaves of a massive oak tree.

At thirty-one Jones was young to be the principal of one of the largest high schools in the state. He'd been picked for his ability, ambition, and drive.

His opening comment was, "How could you possibly assault a student?"

"Hold it." I held up my arm. "What does this look like to you?"

"Bluefield said you attacked him, and he was just defending himself. The two kids who saw the end of the fight say you threw Bluefield across the room."

"What about the student teacher?"

"Who?"

"A woman from Lincoln University. I've seen her around. Bluefield bloodied her nose and cut her lip. Or doesn't she count?"

He looked doubtful. "She never came to the office. Are you sure you aren't making this part up?"

10

This was the first administrator I'd met in all my years of teaching who wasn't a fool, who knew his job, who was willing to put in the work to make the school better—and now he accused me of fabricating an attack on a teacher. I felt betrayed. I lost my temper.

"How dare you accuse me before you even hear my side of the story?"

"What we do have is the students at the door who saw you attacking a student."

"Was I supposed to let myself be stabbed and slashed into ground meat?"

"We have policies and procedures to follow when a student attempts to assault a teacher."

"This wasn't an attempt," I said. "This was a success." I found myself yelling at him. Not a bright idea, to yell at your boss, but I was pissed. "You know Bluefield's reputation and you know mine. Yet you believe him. What'd you do, accompany him to the hospital?"

"As a matter of fact, yes. I've talked with him numerous times. We've established a relationship. You were one of the teachers he always complained about. Said you were out to get him."

Some administrators use an odd ploy with troubled students. They get the kid to believe it is the two of them against the faculty, social workers, parents, and any other adult who might possibly want them to obey a rule. The administrator then becomes a "friend" to the kid. What happens then in staff meetings is that the administrator announces proudly that he or she never has any problems with the troubled kid. What it really means is they don't have any hassles with the kid, everybody else does, and the principal can blame everybody else for not getting along with the kid. Happens more often than you imagine.

"You ever talk to his parole officer?" I asked.

"I have spoken with him. He, along with everyone else who's dealt with Dan in the past few months, agrees that the boy has turned his life around. We were trying to help him, which you seem distinctly unable to do."

I couldn't believe all these people had bought the idea that Dan had changed. "I've had more success with troubled kids in the past eighteen years than half the rest of the faculty put together."

"I know about your reputation. I've talked with a number of parents, including the Bluefields. They had a lot of complaints about you. They said they've heard that you harass students, especially the ones with problems. That you're the cause of a lot of kids' difficulties."

I responded with icy calm. "If you've had complaints, why haven't you told me before this?"

"This incident seemed to offer the best opportunity."

"From whom did you receive complaints?"

"I'm not going to tell you their names. It would serve no useful purpose," he said.

"The contract says you tell me who they are or the complaints don't get recognized in any way. Since you won't tell me, I assume the complaints don't exist and you're making them up. If necessary, you'll be dealing with an angry union on this, but even more, I can't believe a principal not backing up his teacher, especially in an assault case."

Noise at the door caused us both to turn. "The police are here, Mr. Jones," Georgette said. "You told me to interrupt as soon as they arrived."

Two detectives walked in. I recognized Frank Murphy. I knew him from when he was with the juvenile division. We'd had some fairly spectacular successes with some very troubled kids. We'd also had our share of failures, kids lost to dysfunctional homes, legal and illegal chemicals, and suicides. I'd thought he was on vacation. Turned out he was leaving the next day.

Introductions done, Frank said, "I talked to the kid. My bet is he's lying."

"I don't think he is," Jones said.

"I do," Frank said. He asked me what happened and I told him.

When I finished, Frank said, "First of all, we've got to find

12

this student teacher. Second, the kid's fingerprints are on the knife. I believe Tom here."

Jones said, "I'm sure there will be an investigation by the school board into this."

Frank shrugged. "That's nice. As far as the police are concerned this is a pretty open-and-shut case. The kid's a menace. He's been inside the station more than any other teenager for the past two years. If this goes to court, I know who a jury would believe."

Minutes later the cops walked out, leaving a frustrated Jones unable to press charges right then, even if he wanted to. I got up to leave.

His voice stopped me. He spoke loudly, "This isn't over yet, Mason. You may be buddies with the cops, but the school district will have the final say in this matter." His voice softened. "And, Mr. Mason," he said, "I'll thank you never to raise your voice in this office again. I don't accept that kind of treatment from anyone."

I rested my hand on the doorknob. I didn't dramatically shout "Fuck you, go to hell, drop dead." Nor did I apologize. I gazed at his youthful face and said, "I feel sorry for you." If I hadn't banged the door shut, my studied calm might have been more effective.

In the outer office all the lights were out. Through the glass walls I could see Georgette in the hallway, waiting for me.

She wore a light sweater and clutched her purse in her right hand. Her glasses dangled from a chain around her neck. She fluttered to my side. "I heard your voices," she said. "I wasn't trying to eavesdrop, but you were both so loud. He better not try to get rid of you, Mr. Mason. He'll have a tough time. The union won't let him get away with it. Let me know if I can help."

I'd been so angry, I hadn't realized how loud we'd been. I said, "Thank you, Georgette. That's very kind."

She moved her head closer, so her lips were only an inch or so from my ear. "I'm scared of him, Mr. Mason. I think he wants to get rid of me. I'm not young and pretty, and I'm sure that's what he wants."

I patted Georgette's arm encouragingly. She might have had a befuddled act that could win Academy Awards, and at least once a year she got involved in some major office screw-up, but her reports for the state were always perfect, the attendance records and budget items correct to the last dot, and she was a helpful refuge for many a bewildered teacher. She could run almost any computer program invented and knew how to explain each one so that even the most befuddled teacher could understand it.

"I think he'd have a tough time firing you, Georgette."

"I hope so." She clutched her glasses in her right hand and shook them at me. "He's been interviewing secretaries these past few days, but I think he wants to bring in his secretary from his last job. I've done a little calling around on my own." She nodded significantly and moved closer. "He deserves to be yelled at. He's always so nice and polite on the outside, but he's a snake."

We walked down the corridor together. I gave her what words of reassurance I could. At the main entrance to the building she turned to walk out to the parking lot, and I trudged back to my classroom.

The lights in the main hall flicked off as I reached the turn by the faculty lounge. A figure emerged from the doorway. By the light from the lounge I could see it was Donna Dalrymple, our resident psychologist. Through clenched teeth she said, "May I see you please, Mr. Mason?"

I agreed. She led the way to her office which was in the new section of the school.

In the past couple of years they'd finished several new wings. This was the newest and the worst. Its roof leaked after heavy rains and since, like all the new sections, it had unopenable windows, so it was totally dependent on the heating and air-conditioning for comfort regulation. The system never seemed to work right. You might get bitter cold in the middle of September because the air-conditioning decided to stay on high, or you could get Sahara-like heat in early June. The weirdest days were when rooms right next to each other might have completely separate climates. You could step from one to the other and go from rain forest to polar ice cap.

We entered Donna's office. She wore a rust-colored corduroy pants suit over a white blouse and kept her hair swept back from her face in a ponytail. She'd been in the district three years and had alienated nearly every teacher at some point or other. Her basic attitude was that "you poor teachers haven't the faintest idea how to handle these children—only I, a trained specialist, should be allowed to speak to them and deal with them." I generally avoided talking to her.

Nearly every social worker we've had has been a complete gem, brilliant and compassionate, a true miracle worker with troubled children, but according to the rules at Grover Cleveland, the social worker had to take second place to the psychologist.

She tossed the manila folder she'd been carrying into the center of her desk, then faced me with hands on her hips and eyes blazing.

Her office had only interior walls, so no windows gave hope of a world outside. On the cinderblock walls she had posters of rock groups and hot cars. Maybe these made the kids think she was with it and relevant.

She said, "What was the meaning of your attack on Dan Bluefield?"

"I just went through this with Jones."

She rapped her knuckles on the desk top. "You may have destroyed that boy for the rest of his life."

My guilt at what I'd done fled, and total anger returned. I said, "That 'boy' is nearly a man, and he's had far worse happen to him than I just did."

"He's turned his life around. He's reformed. Everybody but you seems to have noticed. What's your problem?"

"Dan is the one with the problem. I can't believe he's convinced everyone that he's now a model citizen."

"I intend to see if we can't file abuse charges against you."

I showed her my arm. "Your little angel attacked me right after he beat up one of the teachers. You believed his story without checking it out."

"I trust him."

The whole scene seemed unreal. I wanted to find that student teacher, if only to burst their bubble of trust in a teenaged delinquent.

"I've been in touch with the parents," she said. "They'll be in first thing in the morning. You'll be lucky if they don't swear out a warrant for your arrest."

I walked out on her. I had no patience for someone incapable of connecting with reality. I had my own emotions to deal with about what happened, and she wasn't helping.

As I walked through the gloomy corridors, thinking about my meeting with Jones, my fury increased. I didn't think the district could do much of substance, didn't think I had much to worry about. A glance at my watch told me I'd be late for the game. I needed to make a call to the ballpark in case the game ended before I got there, so that Scott would know I'd been delayed. The nearest phone was in the office, so I grabbed my briefcase and walked back in that direction.

First I stopped in a washroom. With all the activity I hadn't had time to try and get the blood out of my shirt. I took it off and examined the stain. Probably too dried by now, but I'd give it a try. I ran cold water from elbow to cuff on the left sleeve. Some of the blood washed out. Of course the sleeve was soaked, and I'd have to wear the shirt home wet. Not a bright move.

I trudged down the darkened corridors. The last rays of light from the early October sunset streamed through a few opened classroom doors that faced west. It gave the old place an almost golden glow that for the moment hid the peeling plaster, defaced lockers, and blackening tile. The wood paneling seemed soft and welcoming. The dust motes drifted in around me. I breathed in that old school smell of chalk and kids.

As I entered the office, I noticed the door to Jones's office was open. I picked up Georgette's phone. The glass windows of the office let me look out on the darkened corridor. The sweep of the headlights, from a car pulling up in the school's circular drive, gave occasional light. In the dimness I had to lean my head close to the buttons on the phone. I glanced up. A car's headlight beam swept past the windows in Jones's office. I caught my breath.

At the edge of Jones's desk I saw a hand, a white shirt cuff, and the beginning of the sleeve of a suit coat. A few steps closer, and I saw Robert Jones with a knife sticking out of his back and massive quantities of blood soaking through his clothing.

I hurried toward him and felt for his carotid artery, hoping for a pulse. I felt cold flesh and not a trace of movement. I hurried from the room, being sure to touch nothing, and dialed the police from the phone on Georgette's desk.

The beat cops arrived in eight minutes. Soon, the crime-lab people, along with detectives and captains, joined the fray. Murder in River's Edge isn't unheard-of, but it's rare. This would definitely cause headlines.

I listened to the cops exchange pleasantries, explanations, and theories, a few of which had to do with the murder and most with who was playing golf with whom and whose turn it was to buy lunch. The beat cops interviewed me and took a statement. The few people still in the building got called in. The police found custodians, and the football team coming in from practice, but not much else.

Georgette came in at seven. She left a half-hour later, giving a fearful look at the cops and sneaking a tender pat to my shoulder as she swept by. The school superintendent showed up at eight. They hadn't been able to reach her because she'd been out to dinner for her wedding anniversary.

17

About eight-fifteen the cut in my arm began to throb. At eight-thirty two detectives interviewed me.

The tall ugly one was Hank Daniels. The good-looking young guy with the earring was David Johnson. I'd realized early on it didn't look good: I'd had a fight with Jones. But I didn't know, until they told me, that I'd been the last one to see him alive. Plus I'd found the body, and the dank sleeve of my shirt reminded me that I had bloodstains on it. Not a good combination for establishing my innocence.

Daniels began the interview. "We've heard about you. Dead bodies seem to show up when you do."

Johnson said, "The swish teacher who's always sticking his nose in where it doesn't belong."

Not your basic charm-school interrogation. No matter how hard they pressed, I held my temper in check. I'd been captured by the Viet Cong and held captive for two days. I'd managed to escape, but the memory of the interrogation at that time helped me stay calm now.

Around nine Frank Murphy strode in. They'd kept me in the nurse's office. He sat on the couch they keep for the kids to lie down on. I stayed in the swivel chair behind the desk.

"You're in deep shit," he said.

"Daniels and Johnson were no sweat," I said.

"Sweat is not the problem. You are prime suspect number one. Did you do it?"

"It's bad enough you've got to ask?"

He gazed at me levelly.

"It's that bad," I said.

"Yeah, Tom. I know you didn't do it, and our friendship will probably get you home tonight without a trip to the station, but it's touch and go. The two of them want to arrest you."

"They've got nothing definite. Did anybody see anything?"

Frank shook his head. "According to the interviews, nobody was near this office after you and Georgette Constantine left."

"I wouldn't bet on Georgette," I said. "She's the last one I'd pick as a knife-wielding maniac."

"Somebody around here is," Frank said.

I sighed. "Do you know when I'm going to be able to go? I'm supposed to pick Scott up at the game tonight."

"I'll check." He came back a few minutes later to say I could leave, and added, "We found that student teacher. She looks pretty bad. She was pretty uncommunicative, but I'm sure she'll back up your story. You shouldn't have to worry about the incident with the kid."

I accepted his reassurances and left.

2

Because of the bloodstains, the police had confiscated my shirt, so I had to stop at home for a new one. I took an extra pain pill to deaden the throbbing in my arm. In my gleaming black four-wheel-drive truck, I opened the window and steadied my arm on the opening.

A few minutes later I was on I-80, heading toward I-57 and the Dan Ryan Expressway. I'd called ahead to the ballpark to make sure my ticket was still saved. Fortunately, what with all the folderol of the last game of the season, they'd started late. I arrived in time for the eighth and ninth innings.

The pecking order for tickets was the same as it is in many major-league teams. The wife of the starting pitcher got seat 1-A in the family section. Scott, not being attached to a woman, used to just give up his ticket. As the years of our relationship went on and he became less closeted, he'd simply give me the ticket. The only problem was that I could rarely get to the games because of my own busy schedule. I like to see him pitch at least four or five times a year. It's fun watching him out on the mound in his tight pants, fantasizing about all the things I'd done or planned to do with his body in our bed. My semiregular presence in the family section caused barely a ripple among the relatives and friends. Scott's teammates liked him and he was popular among the wives. Even when he started giving

20

away seats to people with AIDS who wanted to attend games, it wasn't a hassle.

I settled into my seat, saw him notice me as he entered the dugout after the bottom of the eighth. In fairly typical Chicago tradition, the team managed to blow the lead in the ninth, and Scott lost the game. This was the first time in five seasons he hadn't won twenty games.

I waited in my truck outside the ballpark. Scott was one of the last players to walk out of the clubhouse. Kids and adults swarmed around him for autographs even at this late hour. Patiently he signed every program and slip of paper. As one of the few stars in a championship-starved town, he was immensely popular. Finally, he made his way to the passenger side of the truck, opened the door, and plopped himself onto the seat. He wore khaki bermuda shorts that clung to his slender waist and hips, along with a plain white T-shirt over his muscular frame.

"Where were you until the eighth inning?" Scott asked. "I got a little worried."

I told him the story on the way to Ann Sather's Restaurant on Belmont. When I finished, I glanced over at him, then back to the road. In a gesture I knew well, he used his left hand to knead the muscles of his right shoulder.

"Are you okay?" he asked.

"It's still not real to me yet. I've never been accused of murder before." Over dinner we talked of possible explanations and suspects. We managed the meal without Scott being recognized, an accomplishment in itself. Sometimes we can dine out in total anonymity, and other times we've had to flee from overzealous fans. It seems to be the luck of the moment that determines his recognizability.

I drove to his place. He owns a penthouse on Lake Shore Drive. Once there, we performed our postgame ritual. Every time he pitched in Chicago, we went back to his place and had a postmortem so he could depressurize. Lying on the floor, our backs against a white leather couch, we'd talk about the game, pitches he should or shouldn't

21

have made. We wore similar outfits: white jockey shorts and athletic socks.

Tonight we talked mostly about the events at school. He was equally concerned about the Bluefield incident as he was about the murder. As I told him about it, my feelings of guilt returned.

We continued the discussion as we performed the next stage of the post-game ritual on the couch we'd been leaning against. He lay on his stomach while I straddled his torso. Normally, for half an hour I would gently massage all the muscles in his body, spending at least fifteen minutes ministering to his right shoulder. Then we'd have wild hot sex with only the lights from the city below illuminating the room. Afterward we'd have cookies and milk in the breakfast nook, which looked out over Lake Michigan. Sometimes these evenings didn't end until past three or four in the morning.

Tonight, becuase of my arm, we had to make do with the sex and Oreo cookies and milk. Scott still pulls the cookies apart to lick the middle off before eating the rest. We kept talking about the murder.

Halfway through he said, "You seem pretty calm about the whole situation."

"I know I didn't do it, and I assume they'll find some evidence of whoever did."

"But according to you, the guy didn't have a lot of enemies. It could be anybody, including the Bluefield kid. I can't believe others haven't seen through him."

"Thanks for your faith in my insights. The kid is clever, but I don't see him murdering Jones. The principal was his friend. Jones didn't have a lot of enemies I know about, certainly no one I would consider a murderer. But you're right, it could be anybody."

"So, the police could try and save themselves a lot of hassle and just pick you. No more investigation, and a murder solved."

"Frank Murphy won't let them get away with that."

"Look, lover, I wouldn't put too much faith in Frank's

friendship. This is murder. They'll want somebody and quickly."

"What do you suggest?"

"Are they going to let you teach tomorrow?"

"Why shouldn't they?"

"Earth to Tom: You are a suspect in a murder investigation. So you're hardly someone they'd let be in front of a classroom, are you?"

"Innocent until proven guilty—at least on this part of the planet. Besides, the superintendent didn't say anything to me. I don't think she'd try to stop me."

He shook his head. For the moment I just didn't think I had that much to worry about. We finished our dessert without coming up with any solutions.

Later, in bed, he lay with his arms around me, snuggled close. I listened to the hum of the digital clock on the nightstand next to the bed, heard his breathing, felt the down on his chest against my back.

I found I couldn't sleep. It wasn't the sight of the knife sticking out of Jones's back that kept running through my mind, although that was part of it. The incident with Bluefield replayed itself over and over. I felt monumentally guilty and depressed. I heard Scott's breathing become regular and even. I moved away. I tossed and turned, refusing to look at the clock to see how late it was. I felt myself coiled and ready to spring.

Very little can waken Scott, but when I'm restless and unable to sleep, somehow he senses it. It seemed like hours later when he murmured, "Something's still bothering you."

I mumbled that I was okay.

He turned on the light on his side of the bed. I flinched from the brightness. I turned over and saw him sitting up.

"Want to talk about it?" he said.

"What 'it'?"

"You're tense enough to wake me up. You're ready to explode. Tell me I'm wrong."

"I'm not ready to explode," I said. "It's just . . ." I got up, picked up a pair of my jeans from the floor, and pulled them on. I walked to the windows and looked down on the cars still streaming by on Lake Shore Drive this late at night.

I turned back to him. He sat up in the bed, knees raised, one hand draped on each. The blankets still covered him to his stomach. His blue eyes caught mine, but he said nothing. The man is a master at waiting for me to say something.

I turned the rocking chair next to the window to face him and eased into it.

"I wanted to hurt that boy."

He nodded.

"I wanted Bluefield to never taunt another teacher again. I wanted to make sure he'd never harass another fellow human being. I wanted him to feel enough pain to change his fucked-up life."

Scott watched me carefully.

"I wanted to make up for every bit of frustration he's caused me. I wanted him to know that I was a mean tough powerful bastard who he'd better never fuck with. I wanted him to know what revenge feels like."

Scott's eyes bored into mine.

"I feel like shit. I lost control with a student. I hurt a kid and I feel enormous guilt, and I'm angry at myself for feeling the guilt. I had no business trying to hurt the kid, and that's what I was trying to do once I got the knife away from him. Hurt him and cause pain. And it felt good to hit him. I thought, This is for every teacher everywhere who is made to suffer because of rotten kids. I enjoyed it and I feel guilt about enjoying it." I sighed and repeated, "I feel like shit. On top of all that, it's the last game of the season. We haven't talked about it for more than two minutes and I know how difficult this time can be for you."

For two or three days after the season ends Scott usually goes into a minor depression. He goes from a world of huge crowds, center stage, and racing adrenaline to one of relative calm and placidity, and it takes him a while to adjust. To help his reentry to a more staid life-style, we go to a cabin on the shores of Lake Superior for a weekend so he can totally depressurize. I looked forward to those days with him.

Silence lengthened between us. He gazed at me quietly. Finally, I said, "Say something."

He said, "I'm waiting for you to get to the part you need to feel guilt about."

"I told you . . ."

"I listened carefully to all you've said." His soft voice thrummed. I could hear the traces of his Southern drawl. "You're honest with yourself. You understand yourself. You wish you could make go away a lot of the things that happened today."

I nodded.

"And I wish I could take them away for you," he said. "And maybe you saw parts of yourself that you don't like, or wish were different. I listened to a man who I've seen sacrifice himself for kids for the ten years I've known him. Who I've seen do more than any twenty teachers put together to help troubled and despairing children and families. I think you reacted to a threatening situation in an appropriate way. You wish there was another way to have handled the situation?"

"Yes," I said.

"And what would that have been?" he asked.

"I should have been able to stop him some other way," I whispered.

"You're being stubborn," Scott said, "and you're not listening to me."

I folded my arms over my chest, stared out the window at the velvet night over Chicago, and said through clenched teeth, "I am not being stubborn."

"Look," Scott began reasonably. "It's late. You've got school tomorrow, and you need to let yourself off the hook. I think you need to be a little more honest and fair about what happened."

He got out of bed, grabbed a pair of jeans from the

closet, tugged them on, and came over to me. He sat on the ottoman next to the rocker, took my hand, and said, "There wasn't anything else you could have done. You lost control. So what? The first time in eighteen years. You can punish yourself for that if you want. If you need to feel guilt, go ahead, but I know I love you as much today as I did yesterday. That you're the same kind, gentle man I knew then. You're human, with faults—but I already knew that." He smiled. I felt the tug of a grin at the corners of my mouth.

"As for talking about the game, you're more important to me than any other person or thing in this world, and I know we'll have time together in the cabin in a week and a half."

We crawled back into bed.

"Thanks," I murmured as I drifted off to sleep.

The next day at school was chaos unlimited. At seven-thirty, before they let the kids in the building, we had a full staff-and-faculty meeting with a crisis team. Nowadays, when a member of a school community dies, a crisis team is brought in. This is a group of psychologists, therapists, social workers, and others who are trained in handling emotional upheavals. They travel from school to school bringing their expertise with them.

At the meeting Donna Dalrymple glared daggers in my direction. Kurt Campbell, the union president, and Meg sat on either side of me. As Scott had that morning, they asked if I felt okay enough to be at school. I told them I was fine.

The crisis team informed us that we should try to hold our classes in a normal fashion, to speak about the death if kids brought it up, and that any student who showed signs of stress should be sent to them immediately. They had taken over two classrooms in the old section for conferences with individual students too upset to attend classes.

Carolyn Blackburn, the superintendent, caught up with

me in the hallway after the meeting. Kurt materialized at my elbow.

Carolyn looked annoyed. She said, "I need to speak with Mr. Mason."

Kurt said, "I think a union representative should be present."

She frowned at him, but didn't comment. She led the way to the office next to Jones's, where she sat behind a cheap metal desk. We took plastic-cushioned chairs in front of her. Carolyn had until recently been the principal of Grover Cleveland, and was one of the few administrators I almost trusted.

"This is a difficult situation," she said. "Bluefield's dad is due any minute and he is not happy with you, Tom."

"He should be coming down hard on his asshole son," I said.

"Probably," Carolyn said. "He wants to meet with you. I'd like to be present."

I agreed.

Mr. Bluefield's first comment was "Why is this man still in this school? He attacked my boy. Dan's got a broken wrist. He'll be in a cast for weeks."

"He attempted to rape one of our teachers yesterday," Carolyn said. "We consider that a serious charge."

"He didn't touch her. It's his word against hers. She's probably some slut—"

Carolyn cut him off, "As long as you are in this office, in my presence, Mr. Bluefield, you will confine yourself to proper language."

"We're all grownups here," he said. "You've heard these words before."

"Whether I've heard them or even said them, this is a professional meeting and you will control what you say," Carolyn said.

Bluefield looked frustrated and ready to argue some more. Carolyn said, "What can we help you with, Mr. Bluefield?"

He considered Carolyn's comments. The father and son had the same thin, wiry, tightly muscled frame, but Mr. Bluefield might have had the beginning of a paunch. He had pale blond hair, a bushy mustache, and a ponytail. He hadn't saved this morning. He wore tight, faded blue jeans and a flannel shirt.

Bluefield pointed at me. "I want him fired."

"Mr. Mason is not going to be fired," Carolyn spoke firmly and decisively.

"You're backing him up in child abuse."

Carolyn laughed. "Your son is over six feet tall, and when he isn't suspended or on probation he's one of the top wrestlers in the school. If he'd had any ambition or self-control, he could probably have won at the state level. Child abuse is a frivolous charge. I agreed to this meeting so we could work out what to do about Dan. He will not be permitted back in the school. The student teacher and Mr. Mason may press charges."

Bluefield hardly looked abashed at all. He blustered for a while about teachers always picking on his kid, at intervals mixing in remarks about the unfairness of the police.

Finally Carolyn stopped him. "Mr. Bluefield, why did you want to meet with Mr. Mason?"

"To pound the shit out of him."

Carolyn sighed. "Then there is no further purpose in continuing this meeting." She got Bluefield out of the office and returned.

She sat back at the desk. "Your presence is going to be disruptive, Tom," she said.

"How so?" Kurt asked. He'd sat quietly during the entire exchange with Bluefield.

"Kids, teachers, secretaries—everybody is going to be asking questions. The Bluefield incident alone would be cause enough for talk. The murder is going to cause even more chaos. Are you sure you want to go ahead with teaching today?"

I shrugged. "I don't see why not. People are going to ask questions whether I come back today or in a week."

Kurt asked, "Has the practice teacher been interviewed by school personnel?"

"I talked to her myself," Carolyn said, and shook her head. "She wasn't particularly articulate. She may not press charges. I was bluffing with Bluefield earlier. She's frightened. Not the first woman traumatized by an attack."

"Tom is in the clear, like the police said last night?" Kurt asked.

"Pretty much, but it won't be that simple," the superintendent said. "The murder and the attack together add extra dimensions to the situation. Board members have questions. We've already had calls from parents asking that their children be taken out of Mr. Mason's classes."

"You're going to let the stupid and ignorant people run this school?" Kurt asked. "Your obligation is to protect your staff."

"And I will. I'm just giving you information and a different perspective. Some of them are saying that Tom is a threat to the students."

Kurt said, "Don't be absurd. Either they bring some charges or they forget it. We're not going to be part of a witch-hunt by loony parents."

Carolyn agreed, then said, "At any rate, Bluefield is suspended for the moment. I'm going to recommend expulsion to the board. We'll see what happens. Also, we had reporters around last night, and more today. They won't be allowed in the school. We haven't and won't give them your name, Tom, or anybody else's."

We left.

By noon the lines waiting to see the counselors from the crisis-intervention team stretched throughout the old section of Grover Cleveland and doubled back through the main hallway of the new section.

I caught up with Meg outside the library.

"This is madness," she said as two girls walked by sobbing hysterically. "Have you seen Donna?"

I shook my head.

She grabbed my good arm and dragged me through the

library to her office. "You won't believe what's happening. I know for a fact that those two sobbing in the hallway just now had never talked to Jones. Never knew him except as a man who spoke once a year at the opening assembly. Grief and woe are totally out of control, with kids who didn't even know the man. I think these kids are taking advantage of the situation and this crisis team." She snorted. "Those hypocrites are using Jones's death as an excuse to get out of class. It makes me sick. The way these kids are acting makes a mockery of genuine sorrow."

"Grief can do strange things," I said. "Maybe they're sorry for the loss."

"Maybe." Meg didn't sound convinced. "I know what they should do. Cry with the genuinely grieving and send the sobbing hypocrites packing." Abruptly she switched topics. "Do you have any idea who might have killed Jones?"

"At the moment I'm prime suspect number one."

"Redundant but true," she said. "Since we know you didn't do it, who did?"

"That's what Scott asked me last night. I don't like being a murder suspect. I may have been set up. Maybe even by Dan Bluefield in some way. I'm going to do some checking, see who was around last night, see who had a grudge against Jones."

"I don't know what kind of list you'll come up with," Meg said. "He was a competent administrator and intended to make sure the school maintained high standards. His very competence could have been a threat to some people."

"I know."

Meg said, "I'll try and revive the old grapevine and see what I can find out."

I thanked her and left.

I knew who I wanted to find, and I knew where he'd be.

Al Welman was one of the oldest members of the faculty. He ate at a desk in the English department office every day. I knew what he would be wearing. It was Wednesday and every Wednesday since I'd taught at Grover Cleveland, and I'd been told since long before then, he'd worn his brown cardigan sweater, brown corduroy pants, brown shoes, brown socks, tan shirt, and black tie. Each day's outfit included some outward affectation: an umbrella, a beret, a scarf, a six-inch-wide smile button, a rose in his lapel.

Since it was Wednesday, he'd be eating a tuna-fish sandwich with mustard and no mayonnaise. He'd have a red pen stuck behind his left ear and a stack of papers in front of him. After he was through with them, the student essays he graded would bleed red ink. He ate and graded at the same time. All of us English teachers have tricks to wade through the stacks of papers. The trash can, when no one else is looking, is the English teacher's greatest friend. Welman graded every single paper the kids turned in, taking the concept of dedication to the point of madness.

Welman had hated Robert Jones with an incredible passion and as a creature of habit would have been in the school grading papers during the time the murder was committed. I wanted to find out what he knew.

I found him in the predicted position.

One of the last things Jones had done as principal was announce that he would be revising every English teacher's schedule at the beginning of the next semester. This may not compare with other upheavals in history, like the Russian Revolution and the Napoleonic Wars, but to the English department at Grover Cleveland High School, he might as well have announced World War III.

The head of the department, at three meetings last school year, two meetings this summer, and one meeting a week ago, reassured us that as little disruption would occur as possible. Teachers get into ruts. Some of us teach the same thing for years and are quite content. We feel we've paid our dues and earned those classes of bright seniors and other less fractious students, and here was Robert Jones, after one year and one month on the job, ordering the restructuring of the entire department.

I attended the meetings between Jones and the department head because I'm the union's building representative. I was there to prevent Jones from screwing with the union contract. Unfortunately, I couldn't find anything he did that violated it. I had no real objection to the changes he wanted, other than the minor annoyance of revising lesson plans, something I don't find to be traumatic.

In private meetings with the head of the department, Jones used Al Welman as his example of the need for change. Al was too poor to retire and had only a meager pension to look forward to. By common consent, he got the easiest assignments in the department. The last couple of years he'd had trouble with even these. Most of the rest of us tried to take some of the burden off him. The quarterly paperwork for his homeroom got done on a rotating basis by other staff members. We quietly had schedule changes for the few discipline problems he had in his classrooms. Still, he'd become less and less effective in his teaching every year.

Al and I had met with Jones numerous times. They had arguments and once even a shouting match. It got so that Al wouldn't say hello to Jones in the hallway without me, as union rep, being present.

Yet, I couldn't deny the reason of Robert Jones's argument. He wanted the best education possible for the kids at Grover Cleveland, and they weren't getting it from Welman. I thought Jones could have been kinder in the way he went about his work, but perhaps there isn't a way to tell someone who's been working the same job for forty years that he isn't any good anymore.

I thought Jones reached the point of being inhumane and cruel when he told Welman that he had to teach an "out-of-license" biology class. They can do that in Illinois. As long as you teach at least half of your classes in your major area, they can assign you to anything else for the rest of the day.

I knew trying to teach biology would destroy Al, but I didn't lose my temper until Jones made a sneering crack about how "we all have to be willing to change." I hadn't raised my voice, but I let him know in no uncertain terms how unfair he was being. Didn't have the slightest effect.

After one of these meetings Jones had asked me to stay after for a minute.

He remained seated as I stood near the door. "You know, I'm making these decisions in the best interest of the students. He can't make it anymore."

I remembered gazing at Jones silently as he threatened to be in Welman's classroom as often as possible to observe the old man.

This is one of the administrators' tricks when they don't like a teacher. They come into your class and observe you. Formal observations happen to teachers depending on the school district's policies and the union contract. The observation then leads to evaluation. Numerous and constant observations are a good way to unnerve any insecure teacher, and even a competent person doesn't dance with joy at the prospect of an administrator hanging around the classroom constantly.

"What harm is he doing?" I'd asked.

"You know as well as I what harm. These kids deserve the best education. He isn't giving it to them. I was brought in to improve this school. I'm going to do it."

This statement put it mildly. Rumor among the teachers was that he'd been told to "go into that high school and clean it up, especially the deadwood among the faculty." For the first year his effect had been minimal. To start the second year, he'd put his program of change into high gear.

Despite Welman's dislike for Jones, I didn't see him as a murderer, but his name was high on my list of people to talk to. Driven to desperation, even Al might try anything.

Welman greeted me effusively. "Heard you beat up that snotty Bluefield kid. It's about time that little shit got what was coming to him." He sipped from a cup of tea. The back corner of the desk he sat at held a one-burner warmer that always had a pot of water ready to be heated up for his favorite beverage.

With his age-mottled hand he set the teacup down, and picked up half of his tuna sandwich and took an enormous bite. Al was a little over six feet tall, with wisps of white hair greased down and pulled straight back from his forehead. I watched him chew for a moment. With his mouth half full he said softly, "I'm glad Jones is dead. I hated him. He had no right to harass me that way. I've given the best years of my life to this school and he wanted to throw me out like last year's trash. I hated him when he was alive and I still hate him."

"He gave you a lot of unnecessary trouble," I said.

"Damn right."

Before he got launched into a full tirade against Jones, I said, "You know I'm a suspect in the murder."

He nodded and took another bite.

"I'm trying to find out who was around last night. I know you grade papers in here late some evenings. Maybe you could help me with who you saw, maybe even when they left."

"Including me."

I'd avoided saying that. Welman had a temper and a one-track mind, not a good combination. I'd seen a couple of his tantrums with the kids. Years ago they must have been effective in cowing a teenager. Now even the freshmen laughed when he tried it. He'd do an only slightly milder version of a tantrum with the rest of the faculty, but what we really dreaded was his one-track mind. During a departmental meeting, if he got an idea stuck in his head, he never let go. He could hold a wrongheaded notion, a grudge, or simply a whimsical thought for years.

"I want to clear myself and find the killer," I said. "It's hard for me to imagine anybody I know being a murderer, but it's possible somebody from around here did it."

Welman took another bite of sandwich, giving himself time to think, or maybe hoping I'd go away. Finally, he

34

glared at me and said, "I guess I owe you. You saved my butt more than a couple of times."

I said, "I don't see why you need to do this annoyed-curmudgeon act in the first place. Everybody knows you stay late. Eventually you'd be on any list of suspects. I don't think you killed him, but we all know the problems you were having with him."

"Don't push me," he snapped. "Maybe I have my own reasons for being reluctant to talk. Maybe you've saved my ass, but maybe I think you make a good suspect. Maybe I think they might suspect me and why should I try to protect you? They think you did it. What good would it do me to try and help you?"

"You'd say that if you had something to hide."

"I'd say that even if I didn't have anything to hide. I don't want to be a suspect in a murder. You want to be snotty to me, fine, but then I don't help."

"I wasn't being snotty. I just don't understand the big problem with talking to me."

"Oh, don't you? I'll explain so even your young ears can hear properly. See, I know you tell the other teachers what a fool I am in these meetings. You tell them how stupid you think I am."

I'd only told Scott that, not anyone on the faculty. I began a protest, but he raised a hand to forestall me, and he continued. "I know what you people do to cover for me. I know what contempt you all have for me. I know you all just want me to quit and go away. Not going to happen. I'm going to be here a long time. All I have is my teacher's pension when I retire. That paltry sum is not going to be a lot, so I'm going to be here for years to come. And I didn't kill him. I was up here grading papers. I didn't see anybody else. I didn't move from here until after seven."

I tried to reason with him. I told him I'd never told what happened in meetings, but he refused to believe me, and no matter what I tried to talk about, he'd come back to my blabbing about his behavior in meetings with Jones. I decided to ask Meg to talk to him. They'd known each other for years, and she could sometimes get him to see reason when the rest of us couldn't. As I left, he was already back to grading papers.

Next I walked down to the office to try Georgette. She often knew which teachers were in late. She buzzed around me solicitously for a minute or two; then I asked her who might have been in after six yesterday.

"You're investigating," she said.

"I want to find out the truth," I said.

"I know. Being the prime suspect must be hard."

"Is that what people are saying?"

She tittered. "It's what everybody's saying, but when anybody accuses you of murder, I defend you."

"People are accusing me?"

"Not in so many words, but people wonder, you know. A little aura of trouble around somebody, and you find out who your true friends are real fast. Over the years I've seen it happen to any number of people and for much smaller issues than this. People don't like to be around trouble." She patted my arm. "I'll help you."

I leaned toward her across the counter and repeated my question about who'd been in the building late yesterday.

She thought for a minute then said, "I know Marshall Longfellow, the director of building and maintenance, was here. They were trying to fix the heating for the third time this week. He had some man from the electric company with him the last time I saw him, around four." She leaned over the counter and whispered. "I shouldn't tell you this, but under the circumstances . . . I know he got yelled at by Mr. Jones yesterday for not getting the heat fixed. They had words around noon. We could hear them out here in the office. They weren't as loud as you were after school, but it was pretty bad." She lowered her voice even more. "Mr. Jones threatened to fire him."

"You told the police this?"

"Oh, yes, but I don't know what they decided to do about it. And"—she leaned even closer—"I know Mr.

Longfellow drinks on the job, but I didn't tell the police that. Should I have?"

"I don't know." I thought a minute, then asked, "Who else was here?"

"The football team and all the coaches, of course, but they were out in the field. You could ask them if anybody came into the building." She tapped a well-manicured finger on the Formica countertop while muttering to herself, "Let me think. Let me see." She reached back to her desk, grabbed a clipboard, and riffled through the stack of papers attached to it. "Here," she said. Her finger pointed to a brief list of afterschool clubs.

I saw the chess club, the debate team, and the cheerleaders. Fortunately yesterday had not been an exceptionally busy after-school time.

"Of course," she said, "this doesn't include teachers who may have been staying after school on their own, or who may have kept kids after."

"Thanks, Georgette. At least it's a start."

She smiled at me and patted my arm again. "I'll help you any way I can," she said. And I knew she would.

I didn't have time to talk to anybody then because lunch was almost over. In my room I checked my master schedule and found that Fiona Wilson, faculty sponsor of the chess club, had a planning period at the same time I did.

I knew Fiona Wilson from last year, when I was working on the discipline committee with her; she was the most organized and competent person on the committee. She taught all the advanced physics and chemistry courses. I found her in the science department offices. She wore a gray skirt and a crisply starched white cotton blouse, plus a pair of tiny diamond earrings but no other jewelry. She sat at one of the three desks in the room. Masses of paper overwhelmed their tops, except for brief spaces in the center where a teacher could grade more tests and add to the clutter.

She looked up from grading papers and gave me a brief

smile. We exchanged greetings. Then I said, "I understand there was a chess club meeting last night."

"And you're checking on possible suspects other than yourself."

I nodded.

We hadn't become friends while working on the committee, but we had been on the same side in most of the disputes, and the final report came close to most of what she or I proposed. A few of the teachers had wanted to move us back to the Stone Age in discipline; a few even came close to the idea of torturing the students for misbehavior. I hoped Fiona Wilson remembered the committee work fondly enough to help me out.

Without further preliminary she said, "The meeting ended at five-thirty, before the murder took place. I stayed in my classroom. I wanted to work on the computer with a chess problem one of the students brought in. I played with it for an hour and a half. I told this to the police. I have no witnesses that I stayed here all that time, but no one saw me wandering the halls toting a lethal weapon."

Somebody totally forthcoming. I could be suspicious about that at my leisure.

She said, "We've all heard you're the star suspect. Did you kill him?"

I detected humor in her voice as she talked, but a certain wariness as well. I said, "I didn't kill Jones," then asked, "You talk to him much? He have a lot to do with your programs?"

"Rarely saw him. If he had anything to do with the science department he saw Andy." Andrew Buchman, head of the department. Out sick yesterday; I'd checked the list of absent faculty with Georgette earlier. I'd managed to eliminate six out of the 258 faculty members.

I couldn't think of a nonthreatening way to ask the next question, so I plunged ahead. "You ever fight with Jones?"

Her answer was cold and distant. "I've been very helpful, but I don't want to be involved in this. I answered the questions the police asked. I'd rather not go through this

38

with you, if you don't mind. No, I never fought with him."
She turned back to her desk, looking at me over her shoulder. "I have papers to grade before eighth hour."

That helpful conversation left me with enough time to hunt for Marshall Longfellow, head custodian. Janitors have had strange reputations since the book *Up the Down Staircase* was published in the mid-sixties, and probably before. Nothing the custodial staff did at Grover Cleveland would change that.

I tried Longfellow's office, and the main storage rooms. I found most of the custodial staff clustered in a small lounge on the third floor in the oldest section of the school. One of them saw me and immediately said they were on their afternoon break. The stack of doughnuts on the table looked big enough to last them through the next ice age. Their lethargy led me to the supposition that they'd been sitting there eating them since the last ice age. I asked for Longfellow and got a lot of shrugs. With ten minutes left to go before class started, I gave it up and walked back toward the stairs.

On the second-floor landing I noticed a door slightly ajar. I pushed it open; it led outside to the roof of the gym. I stepped out and looked around. I heard clangs from a room-sized heating unit twenty feet in front of me. I approached quietly. This had to be the housing for one of the many heating and air-conditioning units scattered throughout the complex. The view was glorious. You could see half the south suburbs of Chicago, with the forest preserves and all the trees in their full autumn glory. I wanted to admire the view longer, but I had to go to class soon.

I had to walk to the other side of the structure before I found a door. It was open and I walked in. Marshall Longfellow stood next to a large engine. My mechanical training is even less than that of a bored cow so I couldn't possibly recognize its function or what he might be trying to accomplish in fixing it. He hadn't heard me enter, and the doorway was in shadow, so I hadn't cut off much light. Inside was mostly gloom. Near Longfellow a single bare light bulb glared at his work.

Filth-enshrouded work clothes covered a corpulent body. Nearly seventy years old, refusing to retire, he had a snow-white beard flowing onto his chest, and long white hair forming a bushy halo around his head. His red face and the grease streaks he got from scratching his beard were the only color variations in the mass of white. Think of a demented Santa Claus and you've about got it.

Longfellow alternately stared at the machine in front of him, whapped it with a foot-long gleaming metal wrench, and sipped from a can of beer.

"Mr. Longfellow?" I asked.

He spun toward me. The beer can was gone before he turned fully around. I hadn't seen what he'd done with it. He must have been practiced at sneaking a snort or three on the job.

He squinted toward me. "What the fuck do you want?"

I explained that I wanted to talk to him about what happened after school yesterday.

He said, "I already talked to the police. I got nothing to say. Aren't you the English teacher that they think did it?"

"I was here yesterday, just as you were," I said.

He reached behind him and came back with his beer. He took a sip. "I got work to do, and I don't want to talk to you."

I heard the bell ring in the distance. I left the roof and walked back to class.

3

After school I found Meg. I needed to talk to an adult. In class most of the kids had talked more softly than usual when answering questions. Very few of them volunteered answers today. I wasn't sure whether it was because of what I did to Dan Bluefield or what happened to Robert Jones. On top of that, I was depressed because of the lack of cooperation I'd gotten in asking questions. I needed a friendly face and some information. I got both in Meg.

In her office she moved stacks of books from two beige imitation-leather chairs. We sat.

She said, "I hear you've tried questioning a few people."

"Without much success. I thought they'd want to help out a fellow teacher with a problem."

"Rats deserting a sinking ship, my dear. You're in trouble and they don't want to be bothered. Besides, some of them are genuinely upset that Jones is dead. Many administrators are hated. He did some good things that a lot of people liked. He streamlined the supply-ordering system, so you didn't have to wait half a year for a piece of chalk. He cut down on the number of after-school meetings. He tried a lot of new ideas that many of the younger teachers really liked him for, but he kept many of the older ones happy, too. Most of the time he let them alone."

"Not Al Welman."

"The man should have retired a century ago, and we all know it. Even Al knows it, I suspect."

"Did Al hate him enough to kill him?" I asked.

"I have no idea. Tell me what you've found out. I got a little bit from the gossip grapevine. We can compare notes."

I told her which other teachers had been around the night before and asked what she knew about them.

"The football coaches, the team, the cheerleaders, and their teacher sponsors, I don't know much about," she said. "It should be easy enough to see who went into the building from the practice field. You could check after school.

"Now, Fiona is a strange case. She attended Grover Cleveland as a kid, went away to school, and came back elegant and above us all."

"I didn't know that."

"That's why you asked for my help. I find things out." She poured some diet soda into a mug with bright red letters that said, LET'S PARTY.

"Ever notice how the way she dresses?" Meg asked.

"I thought she wore nice clothes," I said.

Meg sighed. "I forgot. You have the fashion sense of a dead buffalo. Her outfits are perfect. She doesn't wear spike heels or see-through blouses. No gobs of makeup or tons of jewelry. That's passé. It's the way she leans over a bit more than necessary, so that you can see a bit of cleavage, or that one extra button is undone on a blouse or skirt. Subtle things that say, 'I'm available.' "

I shrugged. "I never really noticed."

"Well, anyway, Fiona makes the term 'clotheshorse' obsolete. She's a whole herd dressed to stampede. She's dating a young man she met in Tahiti. They live together."

"Nothing there to make her a suspect in a murder."

"I uncover gossip, but I don't know all the secrets about people's grubby little lives like I used to."

I asked her about Al Welman.

"As his union rep you've gone through the worst with

him in the past couple of years. I know he just got divorced a year or so ago after forty years of marriage."

I gave her a surprised look. "I never knew that."

"Most people don't. My source didn't know anything beyond the fact of the divorce. I don't know what happened. Only met her once or twice."

I told Meg about Al's reaction to my questions.

"You aren't surprised, are you?"

"Not really."

"You've got to remember, besides what I said earlier about rats deserting a sinking ship, Jones was generally well liked. He was one of the few good administrators in the recent past, not counting Carolyn Blackburn, who I think is dynamite. She's the first competent superintendent we've had in over twenty years. But Jones . . . Sure the guy made tough decisions. He had visions and ideas. He was young and idealistic. He wanted to make a difference, and quite often he showed he knew what he was doing. Sure a few old dragons who've taught here from the year one didn't like him, but most everybody else did."

"Tell me about Marshall Longfellow," I said.

"An alcoholic. Couldn't find the right end of a hammer even if you held a gun to his head. Been around for thirty years. One of the ones your buddy Jones wanted to fire. Might have been able to make that one stick. You've got a good suspect there. He and Welman were good friends."

"You get anything on Dan Bluefield?" I asked.

"Only a little, and it was strange. This year you're the only one who's reported trouble with him. His past record is atrocious, but if you just looked at this year, you'd think he was a little saint."

"Hard to believe," I said.

We talked a short while longer, but I learned nothing new about possible suspects.

I wanted to talk to people from the football team and the cheerleaders. I made my way through the hallways to the gym. As it did yesterday, gloom infested the corridors. Fewer lights than usual beamed from inside classrooms:

Teachers were clearing out early in case a murderer still lurked in the halls. I decided to check in the locker room first for any coaches who might be around. I could save myself a trek out to the practice fields.

To get from the gym to the locker room you passed through a tiled passage crammed with racks filled with footballs, basketballs, and volleyballs. Mounded in corners and scattered on the floor, other gym paraphernalia provided dark shadows to the already underlit hall.

Inside the close and humid locker room I heard faucets dripping while I stumbled over loose tiles in the floor. The gym was part of the original school complex and needed repair more than anyplace else. The smell of rotting jockstraps brought me back to my own high-school and college days, when I played football. I hunted for a few minutes, but the locker room was empty. As I stepped out the door back into the darkened hallway between the gym and the locker room, a sixth sense warned me of danger. I thought of retreating to the locker room, but this was the only exit. I inched carefully into the hallway. In the darkness, I thought I saw a dimness I hadn't noted on the way in. An instant later something flew toward me.

I flinched and heard an object race an inch past my right ear. I faced my attacker while I backed slowly toward the gym doors and more light.

Seconds later I recognized the permed hair: Dan Bluefield. Despite being suspended, he must have sneaked into the school. He wore a nasty smile along with a large cast on his right arm.

"I don't want to hurt you, Dan," I said quietly.

"Fuck you, faggot," he said.

I prattled to him with the usual "This isn't going to get you anywhere" clichés. My arm still ached from being stabbed, and I didn't want another encounter. His cast actually gave him more leverage.

I backed away slowly and he followed. My shoulder brushed against a metallic shelf. Quickly I swept my arm along a row of basketballs. They tumbled between us. I leaped through the doors into the gym.

He followed after me moments later. Facing him in the this light, I could clearly see he didn't have a weapon. His initial swipe at me must have come from the hand with the cast. He'd counted on surprise for his attack to work.

"Did you kill Mr. Jones?" I asked.

"I wouldn't tell you shit." He moved closer and I backed away.

"You don't want to try anything, Dan, do you?"

"Not here. Not right now." He moved closer and this time I didn't back off. I smelled alcohol on his breath. He said, "You're going to be sorry, faggot. I know where you live and I'm going to make your life miserable. You will be so sorry you ever fucked with me."

I gazed into his dark brown eyes. I said, "I wish I knew how to help you."

He said, "Fuck you," and began walking away. By the time he got to the other side of the gym, he was running.

I decided to delay my trip to the field outside and detoured for a stop at Donna Dalrymple's office. She might have some insight into the kid's behavior. I didn't like her, but maybe there was something she could tell me that could help. Our encounter yesterday had been a disaster, but I couldn't believe that I was the only one having trouble with the kid. I'd give talking to her another try.

I found Donna on the phone in the counseling office. She nodded for me to sit down, spoke briefly into the phone, and then hung up.

Donna had been at Grover Cleveland for three years, and until yesterday, I'd had minimal contact with her. The counselors, social workers, and psychologist at Grover Cleveland divided up the kids by grade level and type of assistance needed. Most were college counselors or helped kids with schedules. A few concentrated on the problem kids, who, if they didn't drop out by senior year, were almost invariably in my Life Skills English class.

Donna had her ponytail swept into a bun on the back of

her head. She wore a brown blazer with a yellow blouse and slacks that combined the two colors. She glared at me.

First, I tried to make peace. "I'd like to do what I can to help Dan Bluefield," I said. "I think the family is in trouble. I'd like to work with you to help them. Yesterday everybody was under a lot of strain."

Her response was to continue staring at me angrily. I explained my most recent encounter with Dan Bluefield.

Finally she spoke, "Half an hour ago, before this attack you claim happened, he told me you tried to molest him yesterday, and that's why he attacked you. I've been on the phone since then to find out what I can get done to you legally."

"What Dan says occurred and what *did* happen are two very different things," I said. "Did you think to come and ask me about it?"

I got a haughty stare for such a ridiculous suggestion.

I said, "It would seem to be a logical thing to do. Why would you take a kid's word without consulting the teacher?"

For a moment I thought she got a guilty look on her face, but a second later she spoke angrily. "I would thank you not to tell me how to do my job. I've already spoken with Carolyn Blackburn. She refused to take any action. You are lucky she trusts you. She told me I had to come up with some concrete proof. Don't think I won't try."

I realized how lucky I was to have a solid relationship with Carolyn Blackburn, but Dalrymple was still talking, "Beyond that, I've spoken with Dan's parents. You had the older sister in class five years ago. You picked on her too."

"I caught her selling drugs in school," I said. "I turned her in. Maybe I shouldn't have, but she had Dan's same basic attitude, which is 'Screw you and stay away from me.' She gave me little choice."

"Nevertheless, the father told me you've been unfair and after his kids for years."

"The father has attended numerous court proceedings with both kids, and he continues to excuse them and blame everyone else. He's out of his depth in dealing with kids who are out of control. You ever met the mother?"

"No," she admitted.

"Neither has anyone else, although she's listed as living in the home. I know they aren't divorced. Why is she never brought into these situations? You and the father have been bamboozled by some kid. I blame both parents, one who doesn't seem to care and the other who can't control his kid."

"You can blame everyone else for your own failures to cope with him."

"I admit I failed with him in class. I'm sorry I hurt him last night, but I know the good I can do with difficult kids. If you don't know that, you should."

"I've talked with one or two of the other support staff. They say you're wonderful. I have yet to see any evidence of it. The point is, Dan hates you and it's your fault."

"Did you ever ask him why he hated me?"

"Yes."

"And he said?"

"You pick on him."

"Try again," I said. "He walked into that classroom at the end of August hating me. I didn't even remember his sister. It'd been five years. I've been teaching so long that once they graduate most of the kids begin to blur in my memory. If they don't do something astonishingly memorable, I forget them."

"And turning a kid in for drugs isn't memorable?" she demanded.

"Do you have any idea how many busts we have here? Can you guess how many kids are selling drugs, much less doing them? If you don't, you should, especially someone in your position."

Her face hardened into a nasty sneer and she said, "You are harmful to children."

For the moment I kept my temper. I said, "I'll tell you why he hates me. He figured out I'm gay, and he's excessively homophobic."

"He's had sex with girls. He's not gay. Why should he hate you for that?"

I gazed at her evenly. "Maybe you're not prejudiced," I said, "but it is unfortunately far too close to normal in this society, for teenage boys especially, to be homophobic to the point of violence. I can't believe you don't know that. What I find truly incredible is that you and almost everybody else around here has bought his current performance."

"You aren't a psychologist, so I don't expect you to understand, and I'm not sure having a gay person for a teacher is good for him."

I laughed at her. "Ask his other teachers before this year, most of whom are straight, how they got along with him. It's the same story as mine, usually worse. I have no idea why Dan thinks I'm gay. I'm not sure I care. Kids can hear rumors, and I don't make a secret of it among the faculty."

"You've been unfair to him, and I believe him. This latest outburst that you claim happened is coming out of your hatred for him."

Why I didn't lose my temper, I'm not sure. I said "You know what happened to the student teacher, and you still believe Bluefield?"

She said, "Dan explained all that to me. He said that she was after him to have sex. When he turned her down, Clarissa went crazy. My understanding is that she isn't going to press charges, which would seem to bear out my contention. Dan says Clarissa was afraid he might turn her in and ruin her career."

"You really bought all that?" I asked.

"Yes. And you'd better understand that I hold you responsible if he returns to his previous behaviors. We've had him in a fantastic drug rehab program. He's been clean for six months, on his way to overcoming child abuse and a negative home environment. It's your fault if all that hard work comes to nothing."

I stood up, shook my head at her, and left. I felt even

more sorry for her. I've seen people get twisted and screwed up about a kid, but I've never understood it.

I trudged out to the practice field. Kurt Campbell blew a whistle at a mingling group of kids. He called them over and spoke to the huddled mass for a moment. They returned to their corner of the field and lined up opposite each other. In various other corners teenagers clad in red-and-white football uniforms participated in various drills, observed by adults carrying clipboards and whistles. On the baseball field in the distance, the cheerleaders bounced and twirled.

Kurt saw me and motioned me over. Besides his duties as teacher and union president, he's one of the assistant football coaches.

I thanked him for being there in the meeting with Mr. Bluefield.

"How was your day?" he asked. "I assume there's no word on the killer."

"No. I need to talk to you, or to whoever knows if anybody went into the school during practice yesterday."

"Probably not a lot of people," he said. "I should have thought of it when I talked to you this morning. The best person to talk to is probably Herman Matusi, a senior. He's the team manager. Runs chores for the coaches. Watches the equipment. He's the brightest kid out here. Too bad he weighs a hundred and ten pounds. I don't remember any of the coaches going in. If anybody would notice, he would."

I talked to Herman. He reported that none of the team had gone in.

"Don't they have to go to the john?" I asked.

He pointed to the concessions stand under the bleachers. "We just use that. It's got a water fountain too."

Out to the cheerleaders I roamed. The weather held beautiful. I hoped it would be this good in a week and a half for Scott and me. For now it was perfect for long walks in the woods, making love, and enjoying the peace and quiet.

I got the attention of the cheerleading sponsor. She gave

me a sour look, issued a few commands to one of the senior girls.

"We're busy," she snapped when she got near me.

I remembered her as Denise Flowers, a teacher of classical languages who had been in the district two years. She looked tan and athletic in sweat shirt and tight spandex shorts. She had long red hair and a figure I think nongay men would find very sexy.

"I wanted to ask—" I began.

She cut me off. "The police asked questions. We quit practice at five yesterday. The girls showered and then I waited for the last one to leave on the bus, the way a faculty advisor is supposed to. None of them left my sight. I was there all the time." She turned her back on me and marched back to the kids.

I decided to give up and go home. I live in a farmhouse in one of the last cornfields in southwestern Cook County. I own the house and two acres around it. I enjoy the quiet and solitude. Last year they put in a subdivision a half-mile from my place. I'm going to have to move soon.

I found Scott sprawled on the couch in the living room. He always spends the first days after the season at my place, to avoid the jangling phones and hectic pace of the city. He wore faded blue jeans, white athletic socks, and no shirt. I noted his end-of-year baseball tan. The deep bronze on his arms stopping abruptly at the elbow where his baseball uniform started, then starting again at his neckline. He'd fallen asleep with a book open on his chest. It was Allan Bérubé's *Coming Out Under Fire*. On the day after he pitched, Scott usually tried to take an extra nap sometime during the afternoon.

Quietly as I moved, he woke when I crossed the room.

As he sat up, the book fell to the floor. He retrieved it and said, "How's my favorite murder suspect?"

"I've got a couple of people I'd like to line up and blast with a machine gun."

"That bad at school?" he asked.

50

"Not as bad as I thought." Sitting next to him on the couch, I told him about my day.

When I finished he said, "I'm worried about the threat from the Bluefield kid. The father is nuts. The son is unstable. I don't like that part about him saying he knew where you lived."

"We've got the alarm system you installed," I said. Scott can do anything mechanical. When he's done fixing things, they actually work.

"He could do something crazy," Scott said. "An alarm system is only so good. I think we should stay at my place for a while."

"Probably not a bad idea." I leaned my head back on the couch. "I'm really depressed about all this. Not about being a murder suspect, because I know I didn't do it, but about the reaction of the faculty. I mean, my friends were great, but some of the others were just like Meg said, rats deserting a sinking ship."

"Trust Meg," Scott said. They knew and liked each other. "You can't really blame the people. They don't want trouble."

"I do blame them," I said petulantly. "They should want to help."

"Am I listening to the man I've heard decree numerous times that people need reality fixes?"

"I'm just frustrated," I said.

"Let's go talk to some of these other people tonight," he said. "You can't stop asking questions. Somebody did it. You're right, someone could be trying to frame you."

"It's kind of hard to believe. I don't have any major enemies on the faculty. In the English department we get along pretty well. I don't know that many people outside the department well enough for them to build that kind of hate."

"What about Bluefield?"

"I don't think the kid has the smarts or the courage to commit murder. Besides, Jones was his big buddy. Why try to hurt him?"

"He had the courage to attack *you,*" Scott said.

I didn't have a good answer for that. We agreed to go out after we ate, to try and talk to the rest of the people who'd been in the school.

I tried cooking some dinner. Neither of us is very good at it, but what's to making pasta? Boil a little water, open a jar of sauce, heat a little garlic bread, toss a salad. The pasta boiled over on the stove and the burner chose to short out from the excess water. When I shoved the garlic bread in the oven, I let go of the door too soon; it crashed down and one of the hinges snapped. Hearing the noise, Scott entered the kitchen.

"This is not my day," I said.

"Hasn't been your week, so far," he muttered. He took the bread out of my hand, placed it on the counter, and steered me to a kitchen chair. While he put the kitchen back in order, I gazed at the *Lord of the Rings* poster-calendar he'd given me for my birthday this year. Finally Scott handed me the lettuce and the knife. "See if you can cut this without slicing off a finger," he said.

I wanted to be more amused for him, but I was too depressed. He managed to forget the sauce on top of the stove while he was fixing the oven door. It burned and crusted on the bottom of the pan.

When he finally plopped spaghetti on my plate he said, "Another gourmet meal at the Mason household."

While we ate, we discussed the recently completed baseball season. He might go to some of the playoff games in California after we got back from our weekend away.

We decided to begin our round of evening conversations with the student teacher. I hadn't seen her in school. I found her name on the faculty and staff list right after the part-time custodians. I drove Scott's Porsche to her place in River's Edge.

We found her house on 149th Street, just west of a recently built bowling alley. A handsome man in his mid-twenties answered our knock. He wore white sweat pants and a sleeveless T-shirt with ILLINOIS STATE UNIVERSITY printed on the front. I told him we wanted to talk to Clarissa. He stared hard at Scott. "Aren't you . . . ?" he began.

Scott nodded. The dreaded recognition issue. Going out in public is a chancy business. He's been on enough posters, been interviewed by enough television reporters, been on enough sports shows to be more recognizable than most politicians. Last time we tried shopping in a suburban mall, he was mobbed. We wound up running for the parking lot, trailing fans behind us. Other times, we've strolled through huge crowds totally unnoticed. The younger the fan, the more tolerant Scott is. He's one of the few major-league players who doesn't charge for his signature.

"No shit, Scott Carpenter," said the guy.

"Who is it, Ralph?" Clarissa appeared behind him. She saw me. "I don't want to see him," she said.

He looked back at her in some confusion. "This is Scott Carpenter," Ralph said.

"Who?" She'd only seen me. Now she took in Scott. No glimmer of recognition appeared on her face.

"Scott Carpenter, the baseball player. I always wanted to meet him." He turned to us, opened the door, and invited us in.

"I don't want . . ." she began.

Before she could complete her protest, we were inside the door. She stomped off farther into the house. Ralph shook Scott's hand. I introduced myself.

Ralph led us into the living room. The house was upper-class track, but the sparse furnishings reflected the newness of their marriage. A picture window looked out on a backyard with trees still small enough to need stakes to keep them from bending over in the wind. We sat on a brown sofa that would need a huge dumpster in another year or so.

Ralph gushed at Scott for a few minutes. Scott's used to it, and performed the rituals graciously. Ralph was about five feet seven, with a wrestler's compact body, as if the gym outfit he wore reflected actual workouts rather than simple style preference.

Eventually we got around to the purpose of our visit.

Ralph's face quickly changed from delight at meeting Scott Carpenter to grim seriousness. He lowered his voice. "Clarissa's been pretty upset. She didn't go to school or to her classes. I tried to talk to her. I don't think she's mad at you. I think you just remind her of what happened. She could barely talk to the police when they interviewed her."

I said, "I don't want to make anything worse for her. If it will just upset her, we can go. Mostly I wanted to see if she was all right. And if possible, to check on what happened with the kid who attacked her. I was curious to know if she'd seen the school principal before he was murdered."

"I don't think she knows anything about that," Ralph said. "But don't leave. Look, I'll go talk to her."

He left the room. Moments later we heard voices from somewhere deeper in the house.

"I can't. I won't," were the only words we heard clearly.

Minutes dragged on beyond fifteen. When it got to thirty minutes, I wanted to leave, but felt awkward searching through their house for them.

Five minutes later they both entered the room. We rose as they walked in. She strode toward us purposefully. She said, "I am not going to discuss what happened. He tried to rape me. I don't know if I'm going to press charges. I don't know if I want the humiliation. I've said this much to please Ralph. Now go."

"Why didn't you at least send help?" I asked.

She looked angrily at me. "I wanted to get out. Get as far away as I could."

She didn't apologize for not sending help, and I had no intention of intruding on her pain. At the door Ralph apologized profusely. He said, "I'll try and get her to talk to you."

We left. In the car Scott asked, "Is the fact that she's not pressing charges going to make it easier for Bluefield's dad to make a case against you?"

"I don't know. I hope not."

"Now where?" he asked.

"I talked to most of the people at work today. I'd like to try Marshall Longfellow again."

Longfellow lived in River's Edge, near the train station. We drove up to a gray brick two-story home. He answered our knock himself and let us in. We saw a great deal of the mass of red veins inhabiting the whites of his eyes as he stared at Scott. My lover introduced himself, and Longfellow continued to stare.

I gently nudged the man toward the interior of the house. We walked through an entryway crammed with boots, overcoats, hats, gloves, random tools, even a rusting snowblower in the corner.

This opened into a living room. A sleepy cat stretched itself across the floor and disappeared around a corner. Longfellow plopped himself into a cloth-backed easy chair. He motioned for us to sit. Looking around the room, I saw that the drapes covering the front window were water-stained and torn. The couch we sat on had been recovered from the dumpster Ralph and Clarissa would soon be bringing their sofa to. Cat hair and fur balls spaced themselves randomly around a carpet that at one time might have been pleasantly gold.

"Scott Carpenter," he managed to gasp at last. "Mr. Mason, how do you know him? Why are you here?"

Scott said, "We live together. We're—"

Longfellow shook his head, "Mr. Mason, you live with a famous baseball player. I don't believe it. I didn't know that. Wow, that's incredible. Can I get an autographed baseball?"

Scott had been about to say that we were lovers. Scott's being gay didn't seem to be much of an issue any more. As his best friend on the team said, "Do you really think people don't know?" I went to his team functions and he came to faculty parties whenever they included the bringing of significant others. This happened rather less than one might suppose. School functions being inherently boring, most significant others didn't bother to attend, and team functions were few and far between. Scott has an enormous speaking schedule that takes him around the country, but I'm usually stuck in the classroom.

So far the local media hadn't seen fit to place our relationship in the sports pages or the gossip columns. If you want to know why not, you'll have to ask them.

Poor Marshall Longfellow simply gaped at us.

"I wanted to ask questions about yesterday afternoon," I said.

He gulped and stared at me. "Yesterday afternoon?" He began to look stubborn.

Scott said, "It would really help, Mr. Longfellow, if you could tell us who was there besides yourself, if you heard or saw anything suspicious."

Longfellow nodded. "If I can help," he said. He offered us drinks. I took a diet soda and Scott accepted a beer. Longfellow chugged on a pint bottle from one side of his chair, and from a beer can on the other. He looked to be functioning as well as he ever did at school. This wasn't saying much—only that he seemed lucid for the moment.

"Did you see anybody yesterday between five-thirty and six-thirty?" I asked.

He placed the liquor bottle on the left side of the chair and clutched the beer bottle tighter. He said, "I saw that chess-club lady, Fiona What's-her-name, lurking in the halls. She doesn't seem to ever leave. She must not have much of a home to go to."

I considered the squalor around me. Great to be in a position to judge.

"Anybody else?"

"All the day-shift custodians went home at the regular time. I was with the night shift waiting for some supplies by the back door most of the time. Some of the kids are always roaming the hall. I think I remember seeing the Bluefield kid."

"What time was this?" I asked.

"Pretty close to six, I think. It could have been him. Whoever it was looked like he had a cast on his arm."

"Bluefield was still around," I said. "He must have been talking to Dalrymple."

Longfellow mumbled on for a while longer, but we got no further information from him. Scott got an autographed baseball out of the car and gave it to him. He carries around a supply of them.

We decided to stop at the River's Edge police station, then call it a night. I wanted to talk to Frank Murphy. From seeing him yesterday I knew he had the four-to-midnight shift. We found him in the squad room, working on reports. Only a few cops were around and none of them made a fuss over Scott. Frank had met Scott often before, so he didn't find it necessary to gush.

"It's good you came in," Frank said. He sounded grim.

"What's wrong?" I asked.

"Plenty. Dan Bluefield says he saw you outside the school office ten minutes before you called in."

"That piece of shit," I said. "All that proves is he could have done it."

"How'd he know the correct time?" Scott asked.

Frank shrugged. "Kid doesn't say, but it wouldn't be hard to guess from when all the commotion started. Just back up the times. Remember, we can't pinpoint the exact moment Jones was killed. There was nearly half an hour between when Tom left and when he came back and found the body. I wish I had the case—it would be no problem. But Daniels and Johnson are tough. I don't think they'll do anything unfair, but they don't know you like I do. I know you didn't do it, but they have to go on the evidence. I've talked to them, and they know Bluefield's reputation, so it should be okay."

"Should be?" Scott asked.

At that moment Daniels and Johnson walked in. They chatted with Frank a few minutes, then asked if they could talk to me. Meeting Scott did not deter them from the questions they wanted to ask.

For an hour and a half we sat in a windowless gray

cubicle while they went over my statement from the day before, line by line and comment by comment.

When we finished Johnson said, "You had the time to kill him, and you've got no alibi."

"Look—" I began.

"No, *you* look," Daniels said. "The blood on your shirt matches Jones's."

"Maybe we have the same blood type," I said.

They didn't even bother to respond to this but went on firing questions at me.

Finally I asked them if they were charging me with murder. They both said no, but they didn't sound any too happy about not doing it. I made an awfully good suspect. Arguing with the future corpse, last one to see him alive, finding the body, blood on my shirt, all very nasty things that would make any cop suspicious.

I found Frank and Scott in Frank's office. I slammed the door shut behind me and kicked a chair against the wall. Each tried to calm me down. Frank said he would talk to Daniels and Johnson again, but that I was to try to stay calm. He was going on vacation for two weeks, but he gave me his number in case things got worse.

In the car I managed to nearly dent the dashboard of the Porsche the third time I swung my fist down on it.

Scott is generally the calmer one in our relationship. It takes me a while to lose my temper, and my rages can be fairly spectacular, but I've calmed down a lot in the last few years. Getting old does that, I guess. Scott's known in the sports pages as the Ice Man. That calm exterior is tough on opposing batters. I've seen him lose it only on rare occasions. He spent the time in the car letting me rant, not even trying to calm me down.

Halfway home I said, "It's late, but we need groceries. It can't wait. We're out of toilet paper, orange juice, a couple of other basics."

I hate taking him grocery shopping. If he survives unrecognized, he is a menace, worse than a little kid, throwing perfectly useless items into the cart. Stuff he's never going to eat, much less have the time or expertise to cook. We've ruined enough meals together to write the *Don't Try This Cookbook*. I try to get any basic grocery shopping done without him. He's only a problem with food. He's fine in a mall with clothes, appliances, whatever. Tonight we were both subdued, managing to exit the Omni store on 159th Street with the only slightly odd item a package of mixed vegetables featuring okra, broccoli, and onions.

At my place I turned off the car. I left the window open and stuck my elbow on the door. The cool autumn breeze brought lingering whiffs of the smell of burning leaves.

He squeezed my arm gently. "You'll get through this," he said.

"The kid out and out lied. I wasn't anywhere near the fucking office at that time."

"I know," he soothed.

"And the cops seemed to believe the little fucker. The little piece of shit is deliberately trying to ruin my life, and there's nothing I can do about it."

"Easy," Scott said. "I'm here. Nothing bad's going to happen as long as I'm around." His support and his soothing tones calmed me down.

We keep a set of weights in my basement so we can work out together. He hadn't started on his off-season exercise schedule yet, and it was too soon after pitching for him to go full-out, but he did a light set. In deference to my still-sore arm, I punished the stationary bicycle for half an hour. After showering and dressing I grabbed a diet soda and moseyed to the living room to wait for him to finish his shower. I left the lights off and stared out the picture window to the moon-drenched fields of corn. I'd seen the big harvesters working early that morning on the crop across the road. They'd probably move over here tomorrow or the next day.

Scott padded up behind me in his stocking feet. He placed his chin gently on my shoulder. "Come to bed," he said.

"In a minute," I said.

He put his arms around me. I felt his chest, thighs, and legs against my back. He rubbed his five o'clock shadow gently against my cheek.

"Don't let it get to you," he said.

"I didn't kill anybody," I said.

"We both know that. So the cops were a little gruff. It's no big deal."

"It's only because of Frank that I'm not in jail," I said.

"It's going to be all right," he said.

I began to turn toward him when a sudden flash from the fields caught my eye. I swung back.

"What?" he asked.

"Something's out there," I whispered.

He stared out the window. "I don't see anything."

"Hush. Let's move away from here slowly. We probably can't be seen, because there's no light behind us, but let's be careful." We edged away from the window.

"Your imagination's getting the best of you," Scott said.

Carefully I positioned myself so I could see over the windowsill.

4

I scanned the cornfield carefully, left to right and back. No sign of life. I hurried to the bedroom, slipped on some shoes, stopped in the kitchen for a flashlight, and marched into the front yard. The light I threw on the fields barely penetrated the dark.

Gentle rustlings from the wind moved the stalks in random bursts. Excellent cover for any skulking attacker. Scott came up behind me.

"I'm going out there," I said.

"Are you nuts?" Scott said. "If you really think somebody's ready to attack us, then call the police."

"I'm not calling the police. This is my home and I'm not going to put up with any bullshit. If someone is going to threaten me, especially that stupid fuck Bluefield, they're going to know they picked the wrong faggot to fuck with. I'm not afraid of some screwed-up teenager."

"How about if I feel frightened enough for both of us? I don't want you hurt," Scott said. "Don't do something stupidly macho just to prove a point."

I glared at him. "This is my home, our home. If we aren't safe here, secure here, then it's for shit and we might as well pack up our tent and surrender. I will not live in fear. I better be able to go out into my yard on a peaceful autumn evening."

"You're the one who said he thought he saw something," Scott said reasonably.

I was feeling unreasonable and petulant. I watched the lights of cars passing on Wolf Road a hundred feet in the distance at the end of the driveway. I walked to the edge of the cornfield and stood poised uncertainly.

Lights flashed down at the road. A car turned up the driveway. Probably someone who missed a turn in Mokena, finally realizing they'd come the wrong way and needed to go back. One or two cars a day used the driveway for a U-turn.

This car kept coming up the driveway. "What the hell?" I said. It was just after midnight, no time for visiting.

The car was a four-year-old Oldsmobile. We walked over. Al Welman's head popped out of the car. His wispy gray hair seemed more disorganized than usual.

He said, "I'm sorry it's so late. I talked to Meg. I've been feeling awful about what I said to you. I was driving around. I turned in to see if any of your lights were on. If you weren't up, I was going to talk to you tomorrow at school."

We invited him in. He apologized several more times for the lateness of the hour and for his rudeness to me earlier that day. "I feel such guilt," he said. "You've been awfully good to me. I'm sorry."

I told him to forget it. I introduced Scott to him. He recognized the name.

"You live here?" Welman asked him.

"We live together," Scott said.

"You're lovers? You're g—" Welman stopped. "The things you see today."

"I appreciate the apology, Al," I said, "but it *is* pretty late."

"I came for another reason," he said. "I"—he paused—"I . . . I saw something. I may have made a mistake."

We waited for him to continue.

"I was near the office at ten after six," he said.

"What were you doing there?" I asked.

62

"I . . . I was going to talk to Jones. We didn't have a scheduled meeting. I wanted to appeal to him without anyone from the union around. I thought he might be less threatened. I know that might sound stupid to you, but I can't teach that biology class next semester. It'll kill me. So I was willing to try anything."

Including murder? I wondered.

I let the silence lengthen beyond the uncomfortable. Finally Welman whispered, "He was dead when I walked into the office. I saw the light and knocked on his door. It was slightly ajar, so when he didn't answer, I peeked in. I saw the knife and I ran."

He twisted his hands together and continued, "I should have done something. I know I should have, but I knew everybody would suspect me. I would be the one to find the body, a natural suspect, and I hate him so much. The police have talked to me several times already. If you weren't such a good suspect, they probably would have come after me. You won't tell the police I was there, will you?"

I said, "Did you see anyone in the hallway?"

"As I was walking to the office I saw that Fiona person at the far end of the east hallway, walking away from the office, and I think I saw one of the custodians way down the north hall. He was moving away from the office, too. I couldn't tell if either one had been inside."

Fiona or the custodian could have been simply walking from one end of the complex to the other, but I'd talk to them.

"Could you tell who the custodian was?"

"Whoever it was had a uniform on. It could have been Longfellow, but he was too far down the hall for me to be sure."

"Did either of them see you?" I asked.

"No, I was coming from the new section of the building. They were already at opposite ends of the halls they were in."

"Opposite ends?" Scott asked.

I explained the school's geography to Scott. The south wing ended at the far west end of the main hall. At the office the main hall continued but was officially called the east hall. Just before the office the north hall branched off to the left if one was walking west to east in the main hall. The school's geography was screwed up because it had been built in sections starting just before World War I. The newest section, tacked onto the far end of the old south wing, made the place so spread-out that any kid going from a class in the new section to a class in the far end of the old north wing couldn't possibly make it in time.

"Why didn't you tell this to the cops? This makes them suspects."

"I told you why. It makes me a suspect, too, and as far as I know those two have no reason to murder him."

"Did you see Dan Bluefield?" I asked.

"No. Was he around?"

"He claims I was there."

"I didn't see you," Welman said.

"Could any other people have been around?" I asked.

"I didn't see any," Welman said. "Are you going to tell the police what I told you?" he asked.

"I don't know," I said.

Scott said, "We won't tell."

I gave him a startled look. Scott said, "Mr. Welman, how could you leave him there like that? Maybe he was still alive when you got there. It couldn't have happened much before you arrived on the scene."

Welman gulped. He rubbed his hands through his thinning hair. "I know," he whispered. "I've thought about that. I may have let a man die. I . . . I guess I was more worried about myself, and I . . . I was, I was so glad to think he was dead, that the idea of helping him didn't cross my mind. Until later, that is. Then I felt awful. At the moment I only thought that the person being cruelest to me was dead, and I was glad. I know that sounds awful, but it's true."

Scott said, "I understand. Tom's told me about the hard

time you've had this year. We won't make it tougher for you."

The old man left a few moments, later shaking our hands gratefully and saying he hoped his information would lead me to find out who did it.

I wanted to go back outside to examine the cornfields for evidence of skulking watchers. Scott's grumbling about hunting around in the dark annoyed me, but his logic convinced me that stumbling through six-foot-tall corn in the dead of night with only a flashlight was dumb.

After we crawled into bed, Scott turned off his light and rolled over. I asked, "Why aren't we going to say anything to the police about Welman?"

Scott mumbled into his pillow, "He didn't do it."

"How do you know that?" I asked.

He turned his head to me. One eye peeked from the depths of the pillow. "I think he was telling the truth. Don't you?"

"I'm not ready to cross him off the suspect list."

"Okay, don't. But I guessed if he thought we trusted him after he confessed, it might help him. He must be feeling awful guilt about not doing something to save the guy."

"Jones probably died instantly," I said. I'd seen stab wounds before, and this one had looked as nasty as any I'd come across in combat.

"Tell Welman that next time," Scott said.

"Let him feel a little guilt," I said.

Scott turned on his side to look at me. "You okay, Tom?" he asked.

"No, I'm not okay. The bastard is here practically confessing to murder, and you bid him go on his merry way, and we decide to keep quiet about it. I don't understand it."

"Do you think he did it?" Scott asked.

"I don't know. If I wasn't so pissed about the police interrogation, I'd call them right now and tell them. That's the only reason I'm not going to. But let me tell you if they try an arrest, I may have to break your promise."

"You didn't do it," Scott said. "You don't have to worry."

"Well, I *am* worried." I paused. "I guess I'm more shook up about that inquisition than I thought. Sorry. If I weren't so pissed off I'd agree with you."

" 'S okay to be angry," Scott said.

We talked for a while longer, but it was late and slowly we drifted off to sleep.

It seemed like seconds later that crashing sirens and flashing white lights blasted me awake. I reached for Scott, who was mumbling himself awake. I rushed to the center of the house. Threw open the doors to the other rooms. No fire. No intruders. I tore open the front door.

Light as bright as day flooded the perimeter of the house from lamps Scott had installed on the roof. Caught in the middle of the front lawn was a figure staring toward me. Seconds later it was gone. I ran across the grass, realizing after a few steps that I had no shoes on. I was surprised to note I'd thrown on a pair of pants. A few steps into the corn told me pursuit was impossible. No shoes, and the enemy had a million places to hide.

I trudged back to the front porch. The alarm cut off and moments later Scott joined me. Seconds later, we caught a brief glimpse of a car, tires squealing, pulling around the corner onto 179th Street.

"Did you see the guy on the lawn?" I asked.

He shook his head.

"Could have been Bluefield. I don't know. What time is it?"

Neither of us knew. We examined the perimeter of the house. At the back door we found evidence of where the visitor had tried to insert something, maybe a crowbar or a screwdriver, between the door and the jamb. He didn't get far, because the alarm had tripped.

Back inside I paced the living-room floor and ranted about Bluefield.

Scott sat on the couch. When I paused for breath he spoke, "You said you couldn't be sure who it was."

"The fucking kid is out to get me. I am not in the mood

to be reasonable." I glanced at the time on the VCR display. "It's three in the morning and I don't give a shit about proof or evidence. The little bastard will not frighten me out of my home."

"Fine," Scott said, "you're going to go over to his house and beat him to death. In the meantime I'm scared. For you. I agree he probably did it, but we have no proof and you know as well as I do that there isn't a thing we can do. Tom, do you understand? I'm scared. I don't want you or me hurt, and somebody wants to hurt you. We'll be safe in the city. My building has good security."

I picked up the book I'd been reading from next to the battered old chair I usually read in. I hurled it across the room. Scott didn't move. With my foot I slammed a chair against the wall. The pictures on the wall rattled. The one of him and me with both sets of parents fell to the floor. Scott jumped to his feet.

"Tom." His low voice soothed and thrummed at its deepest level. After a few minutes under his penetrating gaze, I eased myself down onto the edge of my favorite chair and hung my head. He came over and rested a hand on my shoulder. After a couple of minutes of silence he murmured, "Everything's going to be okay."

I nodded without looking up at him.

We said little to each other as we made our way to bed for the third time that night. I'd picked up the book and carefully placed it on the coffee table. He'd rehung the picture.

I stared up at the ceiling in the darkness, listening to him breathe. I could tell he was still awake. I thought about the day, kids, murder, and fear. A long while later, almost in spite of myself, I felt sleep coming on. As I drifted off, Scott moved close and placed his arm gently on my chest. "I love you," he whispered.

Early the next morning Scott drove me to school. He would pick me up later. I took my cup of coffee and trudged up the stairs to the library to talk to Meg.

The first thing she said was "You look like hell."

I told her about the previous evening's activities, including what Welman told us. I thanked her for convincing the old man to come talk to us.

"He's susceptible to my charms," she said.

"And you have many," I said. "The worst part of all this is I feel rotten about being mean to Scott. He's trying to be calm and helpful. I just get more angry, and feel rotten about being angry, and on top of that I'm torn between guilt and anger with Bluefield."

"Scott loves you and understands," Meg said. "He knows you're not a saint. As for Bluefield, why are you still feeling guilt about hitting him and hating him? After what he did last night, I'd be ready to consider murder."

"Last night I wanted to hurt him. Now, I don't know." I shrugged. "I know it doesn't make much sense."

She said, "You're right. It doesn't make sense. I wasn't there last night, but I think it was the kid attacking your house. Good thing you have the alarm system to scare people away. You've got to solve this murder nonsense. You get that out of the way and you're in good shape. I can't believe the police were so rotten."

"They were."

"I didn't mean I didn't believe what you said. I guess I meant I didn't believe they would act like that."

"The interrogation was nothing compared to what I've been through before. I guess it upset me so much because they seemed to believe the kid, and I know he's lying."

"If they really believed him," she reminded me, "they'd probably have arrested you already. Are you going to tell the police what Welman told you?"

"I promised Scott. I won't unless I have to."

Switching topics, Meg said, "I've got something that may help when you talk to Fiona." It turned out that Fiona'd had sex with a large number of the men on the faculty.

Meg read my mind. "If she were a man, you'd all congratulate him on his conquests. Because she's a woman, she's a slut." She continued her story. Supposedly, Fiona had bragged that she'd had sex with over half the men on the faculty sometime in the last ten years.

"She never approached me," I said.

"You wouldn't have noticed," Meg said. "You are one of the least susceptible men to feminine charms that I know, and we both know the reason."

"Anyway, why would she open up to me? If the gossip line knows about it, and she brags about it, what's to threaten her with?"

Meg said, "A good portion of her conquests have been here at school. In classrooms, broom closets, anywhere you could lock a door and not be seen. Push her on the issue. I'll bet you get something." I shook my head dubiously, but said if I had to, I would use the information.

The bell rang for class. Meg gave me words of encouragement as I left to teach first hour. Being in front of the kids that day was worse than it had been the day before. I was tired from lack of sleep, my arm hurt, and more of them had heard about what Bluefield had said and done the last couple of days. I found myself disciplining more than usual. Even if the kid who tries something is an asshole, the other kids get restless. The cycle of respect is broken. The relationship you've built up with them changes.

At noon, weary but determined, I set out to ask more questions. Yesterday there hadn't been enough time for me to get to the last person on the list Georgette gave: Max Younger, the debate-team coach. I needed to talk to Marshall Longfellow, and I had another reason to speak to Fiona Wilson, besides the fact that Welman had seen them both in the hall yesterday.

I greeted people in the teachers' lounge and found Younger pounding on the pop machine. I tapped it just above the coin-return lever; a coin clinked inside the machine, and a can of diet soda fell into the bin. I asked him if I could talk to him outside.

"I need to eat my lunch," he said.

"This won't take long," I said.

He grumbled about not having enough time, but he accompanied me out to the hallway.

Max Younger wore a beard on a pinched and narrow face. I knew he starred in all the local dramatic productions at the River's Edge Community Center. He was in his late twenties, with an attractive wife whom I'd seen once or twice at faculty parties. I'd heard he had quite a temper while putting together the school plays. The ones I'd gone to had been excellent productions. Perhaps his standards required him to pressure the kids extra hard.

Before I even began, he said, "I don't want any trouble. I was here. I told the cops that I was working on the sets for the new production. Usually several kids are here with me, but the first performance is next week, and my production, stage, and prop managers were all out sick Monday and some of this stuff has to get done. You just can't count on kids."

"You were here by yourself," I said.

"Hey, I'm out of this," he said. "I talked to the cops. I had no reason to kill Jones. He gave us a big budget that we were real pleased with."

He opened the lounge door and slipped inside.

That had gone quickly enough; I thought I'd try Fiona. I found her in the departmental office, sitting in front of a computer screen. She didn't look up as I entered the room. She pressed several keys and one of the figures on the chess board on the screen moved. She looked up. No one else was in the room.

I sat on the desk next to the computer.

"What?" she asked.

"Fiona, someone saw you in the east hallway the night of the murder."

Her gray eyes stared fiercely at me. "Who's the liar?" she demanded.

"I don't want to reveal my source."

"If it was really a source, and not something you made up, you'd go to the police with it to clear your own name."

"Do you want me to go to the police with the information?" I asked. I met her gaze levelly.

"Why were you there?" I asked.

She drummed her fingers on the computer keyboard. The machine beeped at her several times as she inadvertently ordered chess pieces where they couldn't go. She pressed several keys and then returned to staring at me.

"I'm not telling you anything," she said.

Feeling less than proud of myself I said, "I hear you manage to make a lot of the men on the faculty feel good."

"What of it?" she demanded. "It's the nineties. No one cares. So take your threat and shove it."

"You were there," I stated.

She banged her hand on the computer console. She spoke through clenched teeth. "Look, if I thought it would really help you, I'd tell."

"What do you mean, if you thought it would really help me? That's one of the stupidest things I've ever heard anybody say. What were you doing there?"

"I won't sit here and be insulted."

I said, "It's time to tell this to the police."

I marched to the door. Before I could slam it, she called out, "No, wait."

I halted with my hand on the door knob.

"I . . . please come back," she said. "I don't want trouble with the police. I'll tell you."

I reseated myself on the desk.

She turned off the computer, fiddled with the discs for a minute, gave me a grim smile. "I . . . This is embarrassing," she said. "It's . . . You can't tell the police. I didn't do anything illegal, and I certainly didn't kill him."

"Why were you there?" I asked.

She clutched at the chain around her neck, pulling the tiny gold cross that hung there back and forth over the links. "I talked to him. I left him alive." She paused, her right hand continuing to fool with the cross and chain.

"What did you talk to him about?"

She blushed, then murmured, "He caught me."

"Caught you?"

"Here in the office. I was, we were . . . I was having sex with one of the teachers here, who's not married and who wasn't here Monday night. Jones walked in on us. We had our clothes half off, and I was—" She stopped, gulped, and resumed. "Each of us thought the other had locked the door. It was after school hours. We weren't hurting anybody. I know I'm living with someone, but . . ." She shook herself. "I don't owe you an explanation about that. Anyway, he caught us."

"When was this?"

"Last Friday. He said he'd decide on disciplinary action over the weekend. He wanted to see us in his office after school on Monday. Because he went to the hospital with Bluefield, I had to wait until after the chess club meeting."

"Why'd you go by yourself?"

"It was my fault, my idea. I wanted to have sex here. It added excitement to the whole idea. He was angry that my partner didn't show up with me."

"Who was your partner?"

"I'm not going to tell you, now or ever, even if you tell the police. I'm being honest with you as much as I can. I'm hoping you'll believe me. I can't believe you'd turn in a fellow teacher."

She hadn't wanted to help me the day before, but now she expected me to stand loyally by her.

"What did Jones say?" I asked.

"He wanted me to resign. I refused. He said he'd make the whole thing public, go to the school board."

"What you did may not have been specifically illegal, but it was certainly dangerous."

"It wasn't the first time," she muttered.

"Any kid could have walked in."

"And probably would have walked out without saying anything or causing a stink," she retorted. "Anyway, Jones wanted me to quit. He claimed he was being as nice as he could, trying to avoid a scandal. I don't think he'd told anyone else before he died."

"If he hadn't told anyone, that gave you a good reason to kill him."

"I didn't kill him. I'm being honest with you, and it would make a stink if you told, but I'm also being fairly safe. You have no witnesses to this conversation. I can deny anything I've said, claim you're making it up. I'm helping so I can get you off my back. Yes, I know it doesn't look good, but I had no reason to want him dead. He was actually pretty nice about it. I've had offers in private industry. Many people with advanced degrees in math have. It's not like I haven't thought of quitting. I left him alive. Promise you won't say anything."

"I wasn't the last one to see him alive, according to what you've said, and that would help get me off the hook."

"You still found the body and you had a fight with him. Please, you can't tell. My name might be in all the papers. I couldn't take it. My reputation would be ruined. I've been worried that he wrote something down or left some kind of record. I've been afraid every minute that the police would be coming to talk to me. I've got a resignation written out, but I haven't submitted it because it might look suspicious to quit right now. When things die down, I'm leaving. I cooperated with you. The least you can do is cut me a little slack."

The bell rang for fifth hour. If she was the killer, then my knowledge could be just as dangerous to me as it had been to Jones. I said, "I will leave a record of what you've said, but I won't turn it over to the police unless I have to. I appreciate what you've told me. You left him alive. Did you see anyone else around when you left?"

"No. The hall was empty."

"Did you see Dan Bluefield anywhere in the school?"
She hadn't.

I went back to class. During my planning period I hurried to see Meg. I told her what Fiona had told me.

"You going to tell?" she asked.

"Like she said, she could deny all of it. Welman did say he saw her. She'd have a tough time denying that. I believe

Welman, but a lawyer could give him a nasty going-over. The guy is old and the lighting at the time must have been uncertain, and he must have been a basket case after seeing Jones dead."

"You've got people who are better suspects than you. Welman, Fiona, Longfellow the custodian, and probably Younger."

"I can't prove any of them killed him. I'm still angry at the police for the way they treated me last night, so I'm not telling them anything until I'm through talking to people. If they decide to arrest me, I'll have to tell what I've learned. I don't want to spend any time in jail."

"Could they get you for concealing evidence?" Meg asked.

"I don't know. It's a risk I'm willing to take. They're idiots, and I don't have to put up with it."

She eyed me carefully and sighed. "I think you're making the right decision."

"I'm not sure why I'm protecting her."

"Because you're a good guy with a conscience, and she said she was going to quit."

"I guess. I was going to check in with Carolyn Blackburn to see if Jones told her anything or left a written record, although if he did, I assume she'd have said something to Fiona by now."

"She'd have said something," Meg agreed. "He must not have left a record, so Fiona is probably in the clear."

"Or they haven't found it yet."

Meg shrugged. "You still have to talk to Longfellow."

I glanced at the clock. It would have to wait until after school.

I opened the door to my classroom and stopped. Three items lay on top of my desk that hadn't been there when I left. I drew a deep breath as I neared the desk and recognized the grayish lump in the middle, a dead rat, its head half severed and its entrails splattered from one corner of the desk to the other. Almost absently I pressed the button for the intercom as I walked the rest of the way to my desk.

In the middle of the gore on each side of the rat's head was a picture. The one on the left was a nude female centerfold. On the right was a male centerfold, with the genital section slashed to ribbons.

Georgette's voice came over the intercom. "Yes, Mr. Mason?"

"Has any one seen Dan Bluefield in school today?" I asked.

"Let me check."

The intercom clicked off. I picked up the trashcan from next to the door. Using the spine of my teachers' manual, I nudged the mess from the center of my desk into the garbage. I covered it with several layers of paper.

I was furious. Any guilt I felt for beating up Bluefield was gone. There was no doubt in my mind about whom the rat and the nude pictures had come from.

Georgette's voice came over the intercom. "He's listed officially as absent. One of the kids here waiting to see Mrs. Dalrymple says he thinks he saw him early this morning lurking in the halls."

At my request, she sent down Carolyn Blackburn. I showed her the debris. She lifted a hand to her mouth. "This is too horrific," she whispered.

Carolyn agreed that this needed to be reported to the police. I passed up the temptation to dump the mess on Donna Dalrymple's desk. Before Carolyn left, I thanked her for backing me up against Dan Bluefield's claim.

She said, "Besides the fact that I don't believe you would molest a child, Dan made it tough to believe him when he only reported it the morning after."

Last hour passed in a blur. I did ask if any of the students had seen Bluefield. They hadn't. I think I forgot to give them homework, and the kids were fairly stunned about that.

First thing after school I hunted for Marshall Longfellow while keeping a sharp lookout for Bluefield. Once again the elusive Mr. Longfellow proved difficult to find. I had Georgette page him on the intercom, and he still didn't respond. None of the custodians had seen him for over two hours. We began a search. Carolyn Blackburn, currently doubling as school principal until a replacement could be found, joined the search.

I hunted through the oldest basement of the school, calling his name without getting a response. I explored every corner. The basement was directly underneath the old gym. From the door I could see the old coal furnaces, which had been converted to oil, then to natural gas, and then finally abandoned. They lurked like cold dinosaurs in dank dimness. Add a few shower stalls and this could be the locker room. I proceeded slowly through the room.

Cobwebs brushed against my face when I rounded the huge furnaces. The light became dimmer farther into the room. In one corner, steady drips of water fell from some of the old beams. I guessed I was beneath the shower room. The drips formed into a stream that flowed toward the back of the room. As I proceeded farther, more damp spots appeared on the floor and more drips added to the flowing water. I began to hear a rhythmic rumbling every fifteen seconds; there was a glow in the distance that wasn't made by the sparsely spaced twenty-watt bulbs in the ceiling. The rumbling grew louder. I sniffed the air and got the reek of raw sewage.

I turned a corner behind the last and largest of the furnaces. On a small platform raised above the dampness of the floor by plastic milk cartons was a twin bedframe with a bare, prison-thin mattress on top. On it lay Marshall Longfellow, sound asleep. Mounted on the wall ten feet from the bed was a vast array of gauges and switches along with a blizzard of wires connected to them and trailing off in every direction. The humming noise came from a large puddle just below the electric mess.

The inflowing water from the drips gathered here, but I soon realized the problem was greater than I thought. Every fifteen seconds, when the noise came, water burbled up from the middle of the pool of water. I watched this happen several times, and I realized that at every rumble the water poured in; when the noise stopped, the water receded. But every cycle brought the dank pool an inch higher. It had already reached several of the wires, from which occasional sparks emanated.

I wasn't about to attempt disconnecting anything. The smell from the pool of water was ghastly. I guessed the sump pump was malfunctioning. I'd helped Scott replace the one in my basement, and he'd taken extra care to make sure it was connected right for just this reason. He'd told me some people connected the sump pump to the sewage system: unhealthy, and a violation of the building codes. If the pump backed up or otherwise malfunctioned, sewer water could pour into bathtubs, toilets, or sinks.

Avoiding the pool of water, I shook Longfellow awake. He snorted and snuffled for several seconds, then saw me and said, "I wasn't asleep. I'm wide awake." He struggled to get up.

"Be careful where you step!" I warned him.

He looked at the floor and quickly moved his feet away from the dampness.

"You better do something before this starts some kind of fire," I said.

"We got to get this water mopped up," he said.

"Shouldn't we turn off this electricity first, or at least get the sump pump turned off?" I said.

"Oh yeah, right." He scratched his head.

I moved back a step as the water surged closer. I had no intention of being electrocuted because some drunken fool couldn't find a switch.

"We've got to get to the circuit breakers," he muttered. "We've got to cut the power before the water gets any higher."

"Where is it?" I said.

As he pulled his befuddled self together, I hurried in the direction he indicated. After fumbling around in the dimness for five minutes, I found the control panel. None of the switches were labeled. They were all in the same position, which I presumed had to be on. Tentatively I flipped several of them, not sure what part of the complex I was denying electricity to. If a switch didn't turn off any electricity here, I immediately flipped it back on.

Halfway through my random search, lights in the basement winked off. At first I thought I'd done it, but I hadn't flipped a switch just before the lights winked out. A howl of complaint came from where I'd last seen Longfellow. I stayed where I was and stopped flipping switches. I assumed if Longfellow didn't have a flashlight, then at least one of the other custodians would come hunting the reason for the power failure.

I listened to the dripping of water and the cursing of the custodian, neither of which seemed tremendously imaginative. A few minutes later a glow of light formed at the opposite end of the room. In five minutes the entire custodial staff stood around me and the control panel, flipping switches back and forth, trying by trial and error to see which switch controlled what. Longfellow joined us early on in the process. His years of expertise as head custodian led him to continually comment, "No, asshole, try another one."

Finally, light restored, underlings dispatched, wires disconnected, and the threat of fire eliminated, I tapped Longfellow on the shoulder. "I need to talk to you," I said.

He looked annoyed but followed me to a corner behind one of the grime- and soot-encrusted furnaces.

He said, "You're not going to tell about . . ." He cleared his throat. "About my needing to take a rest."

"I need information," I said. "You talk to me, tell me the truth, and I don't say anything."

He nodded glum agreement.

I told him he'd been seen outside the principal's office on Monday night at the time of the murder.

"No," he said.

"Carolyn Blackburn would love to know about your little nap," I said.

His bloodshot eyes wouldn't meet mine. "I can't help it," he said.

I asked him what he couldn't help.

"I need to calm my nerves," he said. "It helps me relax. I'm not an alcoholic. I can say no. It just helps me. But Jones, that bastard, he wouldn't see it that way. He told me to stop drinking on the job. All last year I stopped. Just once or twice this year I took a sip." Longfellow drew a sharp breath and turned his bleary eyes on me. "He caught me last Friday at noon. I was down here. No principal ever came down here before. He did. I've been here thirty years and him less than two and he was going to put me on probation, like some kid who doesn't even have a high-school diploma. He wanted to humiliate me in front of everyone. Said if I wanted to avoid that I could resign. He smirked at me. I know he's been looking for an excuse to get rid of me."

"Why did you go down to his office Monday?" I asked.

"I had an appointment. I was a few minutes early. It was a short interview. He told me he wanted my resignation Tuesday morning. If he didn't get it, I would be fired at the next board meeting, which is tonight."

"Did you fight with him, argue about it?" I asked.

"I tried, but he said he didn't want to hear it. He said it was real simple. I quit or I got fired. He hadn't told Carolyn Blackburn yet. He was giving me a chance to do the right thing. Pissant little snot. I'm glad he's dead." He glanced at me quickly. "I didn't kill him. He was alive when I left him. You can't tell anyone this. You promised if I was honest you wouldn't tell."

That wasn't exactly my promise, and the man was a hazard: A fire could have started. Or maybe I was over reacting to what I'd seen as a dangerous situation. When Frank Murphy came back, I could reassess my decision not to tell.

"Nobody's going to hire a sixty-eight-year-old drunk," he whined. "You promised not to say anything."

I told him I wouldn't. I asked if he'd seen anybody else. He hadn't. I had no way of telling who'd seen Jones last, Fiona or Longfellow. Or maybe there'd been a whole string of people to see Jones.

When I got back to my classroom, I found Scott sitting on top of my desk talking to Meg, who had been telling him about the day's progress. I told them both about Longfellow.

"So you're double in the clear," Scott said.

"Yes, but I promised not to tell the police or the administration about either one of them."

Meg said, "And each one of them claims to have left Jones alive. . . . You know Longfellow and Welman are close friends?"

I gave her a quizzical look.

She said, "They used to go out drinking every Friday night. A couple of years ago Welman got a scare about his liver, and he stopped drinking. I don't know how close they are now."

Scott said, "Could the two of them have planned the murder?"

We discussed the issue further, but got nowhere. Meg went back to the library. I told Scott about the rat and the porno pictures.

"The kid's out to get you," Scott said, "but we still can't prove anything."

Reluctantly I agreed with him.

"Let's go to my place," Scott suggested.

"I want to go to Jones's wake tonight," I said.

"You sure that's a good idea? The family will be there. Someone might tell them you're under suspicion."

"I doubt if the police go around to each family and announce who they think did it. The relatives wouldn't recognize me, anyway. I'm sure some of the faculty will be there. I'd like to try and talk to a few more, see who might have seen something. This running around school takes too damn long. With a lot of people in one place, maybe I can get more questions asked more quickly. We need to find out if anyone else was around, or if somebody else had a motive."

"I wish Frank Murphy hadn't gone on vacation," Scott said. "He might have some good suggestions about what to do about Bluefield. That kid has got to be stopped."

5

On our way to the car, in the hallway outside the office we ran into Carolyn Blackburn. She didn't look happy to see us. We sat in her temporary quarters. I didn't make introductions; she and Scott had met several times before at various parties and functions.

"What's wrong?" I asked.

"Plenty. The police called. Bluefield's dad was down at the station with an attorney. He wants to press charges against you for attacking his kid. Fortunately, you've got a good reputation down there, and, it seems, some clout. I did what I could to put a stop to it, including telling them about the horrors we found on your desk, but I think the guy is going to try to get a judge to do something. He tried calling a few board members, but they told him to talk to me. That put an end to the nonsense from that end, but Mr. Bluefield is on a personal crusade to see you fired. I wish we could do something."

We discussed the attacks on the house, the dead rat, and the porno pictures. We discussed my staying in the city at Scott's.

"This is so sick," she said. "I think Scott is right. You two should stay at his place in the city for a while, at least until this blows over."

"I keep swinging between fear and anger," I said. "The

dead rat on my desk has me shook up more than I thought. Still, I'd rather stay at my place."

Scott said, "Look, Tom, let's go eat something and talk it over some more. If you really want to stay at your place, we can try and work something out, okay? We'll get through this."

"One odd thing about the police," Carolyn said. "They didn't mention anything about molestation charges."

"Dan only told Dalrymple, but not his dad. Curious," I said. We examined the implications of that for a while, but came up with little.

Before we left Carolyn filled us in on the latest in the investigation. She said, "The police wouldn't tell me all of what they know, but they did say they have the fingerprint report back. Your prints, Tom, along with many others, were in the office."

"I was there," I said.

Carolyn added, "They didn't find any fingerprints on the knife. The killer wiped it clean."

"Not a lot of help there," I said.

"They told me a bit more. It's not good. They asked me about your disagreements with Jones. It's not a secret you and he fought, plus you've got a history of being antagonistic toward administrators."

I started another protest, but Carolyn held up a hand to stop me. "I know it's part of being a good union rep to stand up to the bosses and not be pushed around. You've done a lot of good. I was a union rep when I was a teacher, so I understand. I tried to make the cops see that, too."

"Are Johnson and Daniels going to question me again?" I asked.

"I don't think so. Not today, anyway."

"Maybe I should talk to a lawyer," I said.

Carolyn said, "Maybe you should."

"Is it that bad?" Scott asked.

"It's not real good. They don't have anything to pin the murder on you specifically, but I think they're having trouble coming up with other suspects, and that nonsense from Dan Bluefield didn't help." She frowned and said, "I'm worried about Donna Dalrymple. Not the material she repeated from Dan, but that she believed it so readily. I find her reaction odd, to say the least."

I filled Scott in on my conversation with Donna.

"What's going on between the two of them?" Scott asked.

"I'm not sure," Carolyn said, "but I'd like to find out. What have you discovered in your questioning?"

"I'm surprised Daniels and Johnson haven't harassed me about that," I said.

"I'm supposed to be warning you not to talk to people," Carolyn said. "And you do need to be very discreet. Nosing around could cause trouble."

I didn't break my several promises to keep people's stories quiet. I was still miffed about my treatment of the night before, and while I did trust Carolyn, I wasn't ready to take her any further into my confidence at this moment.

Scott asked, "We were planning on attending the wake. Do you think we'd have any problem with the family?"

Carolyn said, "I don't think so. They haven't released a lot of information to the press, although someone at the wake could recognize you and tell the family. It's not a tremendous secret that you're under suspicion."

"The rumor is certainly around the faculty that I'm a major suspect," I said.

"Be discreet," Carolyn suggested again. "I wanted to give you the information and to tell you to take care. I suppose the police will probably be around to question you again. Try not to worry about it."

I thanked her. As we walked down the hall to our cars I said, "They must have talked to the family. They usually look pretty closely at the wife in this kind of thing."

"I heard she had a solid alibi," Carolyn said. "She works at a day-care center and was there until six-thirty that night. She's in the clear. I know Jones didn't have any other close family around here. They were from Centerboro, in New York."

As we said good-bye in the parking lot Carolyn said, "Be careful of Dan Bluefield. My guess is that you've got more to worry about from the boy and his dad than you do from the murder."

We thanked her, and she left.

"I need to get away," I said as Scott drove the Porsche out of the school parking lot.

Scott asked, "Why not call in sick tomorrow and forget all this?"

"I need to get away right now for a little while, but I'm not calling in sick. I'm not giving up until I clear myself in this murder investigation, and we've got to resolve this Bluefield thing."

"Maybe there isn't a resolution," Scott said. "Maybe it will just take time."

We decided to eat at Cookies in Minooka, a quiet little town a mile or so off the interstate, about a half hour's drive from Joliet. At Cookies the food is good and the atmosphere is relaxed. We didn't say much to each other as we drove. We listened to a folk-music tape I'd compiled from several of my favorite albums. Two hours later I felt somewhat revived and ready to attend the wake.

The funeral home was on Front Street in Mokena, across from the fire station. They'd taken an old Victorian mansion, renovated it, and added rooms in back.

As I reached for the door handle of the Porsche, I noticed a person lurking in the shadows on the west side of the fire station. I tapped Scott on the shoulder. "I think that's Bluefield," I said.

He looked where I pointed.

The shadow moved farther into the darkness. Scott said, "Are you sure?"

"No. Maybe we should check it out." He agreed. We crossed the street and hunted through the shadows, but whoever it was had taken off.

Inside the funeral home twenty-five or thirty people milled around the viewing room. A few near the casket seemed to be the family. I spotted various faculty members and several students. One of these detached herself from a small group and came over to us.

I recognized Sheila Tarelli. She'd been in my Senior Honors English class, the brightest kid I'd had in my classes in the past five years. She had a full scholarship to De Paul University, where she planned to major in theater. She wanted to be a playwright, actress, director, and producer. I had no doubt she would be someday.

She came over and smiled happily. We had become good friends over the year I'd had her in class. I introduced Scott. She gave him the same radiant smile and said, "The baseball player. Nice to meet you." And then dropped the topic of Scott's profession. A few other people in the crowd had noted his presence, but so far, perhaps because of the funeral-home atmosphere, had yet to venture close.

We moved into a corner in the hallway, out of the way of many in the crowd, but where we could still see who entered. We talked about her college classes and several of the kids from class last year, most of whom I still remembered.

Suddenly she gave a little gasp and placed herself so that we were between her and the doorway.

"What?" I asked.

She whispered, "It's Mr. Younger. I don't want to see him. He's poison."

"I thought you liked him," I said. "You had all the major female roles in the plays your junior and senior years."

"I'm taking one theater course now, and I've got a small part in the first production of the season, and in both places I've learned what an amateur he really is. He doesn't know anything about directing. Last year, especially, I thought his method of directing by tirade was totally childish. Now I know it is. I'm not saying that because I've graduated, I know everything. It's just— He was such an awful person. He puts you through hell. It should be hard work, but you should get some fun out of it. Plus, he hates me."

"Why?" I asked.

She moved even closer, still keeping us between herself and Younger. "You can't tell anyone this," she said, "but I caught him last year. He cheats on the account books for the plays. He's been skimming money from the production budgets. He orders props that never show up and keeps the money. Same with makeup, scenery, paint, everything."

"How'd you find out?" I asked.

"I'm good at math and computers—quick—you know."

I nodded. Last year she'd told me she'd been only several points from a perfect score on the math portion of her SAT.

She continued, "He gave me some orders to fill out and put into the computer. I didn't understand the program at first, and I called up the incorrect data. It was the past years' orders, and I thought maybe I could just tie last year's in with them. I noticed the prices and was struck by the discrepancy between last year and the years before. At first I thought it was just some mistake somebody made putting in the numbers into the computer. I checked the catalogue we order from. I thought I'd be doing him a favor by making the corrections. He got real mad when I told him about it. Told me to keep my snotty nose out of his business. He dared me to turn him in. Said no one would believe the word of a kid against a teacher. Besides, he had the computer disc with the proof."

She shrugged. She told us about running into a friend of hers this past summer who had helped Younger the year before. The friend had told Sheila that she, too, had thought something funny was going on and had mentioned it to Younger. He'd threatened her the way he'd threatened Sheila.

"My friend wouldn't go with me to report him or anything," Sheila explained. "She said she didn't want to be involved. There was nothing I could do."

I sympathized with her and then told her about the problems I'd been having at school and how uncooperative he'd been when I tried talking to him. "I'd like to use what you told me as leverage in getting him to talk."

She got a wicked smile on her face. "The jerk was rotten to me. In fact, I don't care if you tell him you heard it from me. He can't hurt me. I hope you nail the scummy creep."

We thanked her and wished her luck in her classes. She went back to her group. We hunted for Younger. I saw him up at the casket talking to the family. Several people reached out and touched Scott's arm and introduced themselves as we waited for Max in the back of the room.

As Max passed us, I leaned over and whispered in his ear. "We have to talk."

He glared at me. "I have nothing to say to you."

"Let's talk about cheating on your ordering."

Briefly his pink cheeks turned grayer than the corpse. I took his elbow, and we entered an unused viewing room. I introduced Scott.

Younger barely acknowledged the introduction. He said, "What do you mean by that rude remark? I've never done anything untoward in the theater department."

"Our source says you did."

"Lies."

"Why don't we go check the records right now?" I said.

"Who told you this bullshit?" Younger demanded. "Was it that Sheila Tarelli? She's hated me for being honest with her. She doesn't have enough talent to make diaper commercials for illiterate natives in the Amazon."

"Let's go check the records," I said.

"You can't make me do anything," Younger said. He turned toward the exit.

Scott moved swiftly to place himself between the theater teacher and the door.

Younger turned back to me. "You can't keep me here," he said.

I grabbed a fistful of his shirtfront and pulled the five-foot-eight man to within an inch of my nose. "Listen, Max, unless you talk within two minutes, I'm taking an accusation straight to the administration. We'll ask them to do a little audit of your books for the last five years."

"Let me go," Younger squawked.

I held onto him tightly, easily fending off his feeble attempts to free himself.

I had a sudden thought. "Jones caught you," I said. "He was competent. He checked over everything. He watched where every nickel went. He devised the new ordering system. Something put him on to you."

His corpselike pallor returned. "He did no such thing," Younger said.

Still gripping his shirtfront, I gave him a shake. I heard his teeth rattle. Younger struggled briefly again. Saw it was futile.

I eased my grip on him.

Younger shrugged his shoulders so that his corduroy sport coat with leather patches at the elbow settled correctly onto his frame. He straightened his tie and tried to regain his dignity.

I said, "I want to hear the whole story, or we go to Carolyn Blackburn tonight."

"Shit," he said.

We waited.

Finally he said, "All right. Fine. I guess it was too much to hope that it would die with him."

The room had five rows of chairs facing the front, where a casket would be placed. Younger sat in one of the chairs in the last row. We turned two others to face him.

Younger loosened his tie, cracked his knuckles, and then told us the story. It started six years ago when he first began teaching. He'd been put in charge of the theater and with no experience except several college courses, he'd ordered far more material than was necessary. To his surprise, no one said a word. It turned out that most of the theater-department ordering went through a separate budget category, was seldom checked up on, and was often done in cash.

Such anomalies in accounting often cropped up in a

school district as large and old as River's Edge; besides, we'd had a series of incredibly incompetent administrators. With Carolyn Blackburn and Jones things had begun to change.

In the past no one checked the amount of money Younger took out of the account. No one ever asked for receipts, and quite often, he found by looking at past records, teachers had simply written the cost of an item on a piece of paper and added it to the budget file. They'd had to computerize the system two years ago, but that still hadn't been a problem. All Younger had to do was put inflated prices in the right spots in the computer. "My problem came when I got lazy. I let the kids enter the figures. I never thought the administration would check. They never had before. I was stupid to let Sheila do it this year after the kid last year caught on. How was I to know they'd both stumble on the same thing? I thought I had the program well guarded. These goddamn kids who are so computer literate make me sick."

When Sheila found the discrepancies, she'd told Younger. He'd gotten angry, which was a mistake, but at least she didn't turn him in. I'd been right, however, in guessing that Jones had caught on.

"He came by the theater office one day near the end of summer vacation," Younger said. "I was in doing some extra work. If I'd stayed home, maybe this wouldn't have happened. Jones said that as part of the new system of ordering, they'd put all the departmental and special orders on a new computer program that the office would manage. I told him that wasn't necessary. I would have told him that the program was at home, but the computer with all the discs was right there. I had to give it to him."

Jones had gone through the system and found all the discrepancies. He'd confronted Younger a week ago, saying that if the entire amount was paid back, the police wouldn't be called. Younger had until the end of the school year to replace the money. Jones said he would take the final payment along with Younger's resignation.

"Jones said if I didn't pay back the money, he'd take the matter to the school board and everything would be made public. I couldn't take my reputation being ruined. I've helped a lot of these kids. They look up to me. A lot of parents respect me for what I've done. I'd have to move. I'd probably never get a decent job teaching theater again."

He cracked his knuckles for the fifteenth time during the conversation. I wanted to break his hands.

"I didn't know what I was going to do. I begged and pleaded with Jones to give me a second chance. The guy had no mercy. Jones was implacable."

"So you killed him," I said.

"No, I swear! I was nowhere near the office that night after school. I admit I was in school at the time, but it wasn't me."

"How much money do you owe?" Scott asked.

"Over six thousand," Younger said.

"How could it be that much?" I asked.

"We have the largest high-school drama department in the state. One of the largest in the country. We've won all kinds of awards locally and nationwide. We've got clout. I took a little over a thousand a year. I couldn't possibly raise the money to pay him back. I had a meeting set up with him next week to discuss it."

"I wonder if he told Carolyn," I said.

"I don't know," Younger said.

"Did you see anybody else in the school that night?" I asked.

"No, I stayed in the theater department the whole time." He cleared his throat. "You know I'm not the only one who was threatened by Jones. There were other people on the faculty."

"Who?" I asked.

He cracked his knuckles again. "I really shouldn't say."

"You've gone this far," I said. "We don't want to cause you any trouble. I'm trying to find out who killed him to help clear my own name. Anything you can tell us would probably help. And you'll be clearing your name, too. You had a reason to kill him."

"Yeah, I guess." He sighed. "All right. I'm not sure about this." He lowered his voice conspiratorially. "I heard that Dan Bluefield is having sex with one of the faculty members and that Jones found out about it."

He smiled with satisfaction.

Sex between kids and teachers was something I could never fathom. I know guys I've talked to, both straight and gay, who said they had sex with teachers when they were in high school. They were happy they did it, and felt no trauma because of it. They were probably the lucky ones. Far too many are unlucky, abused, and hurt by the incidents.

I asked the obvious question. "Who's the teacher?"

He hesitated. "I don't want to ruin another person's reputation if it isn't true."

"We can at least check it," I said. "We need all the help we can get."

He said, "Not a teacher. Donna Dalrymple."

I spent the remainder of the few minutes we talked together being fairly flabbergasted. I barely heard as Scott tried to find out where Younger had heard the rumor. He couldn't remember specifically, but vaguely recalled that it had been talked about in the teachers' lounge.

He left.

I said to Scott, "Sex with kids?"

"It would explain her attitude toward the boy," Scott said.

A few minutes later we left the room. I saw Meg just coming in the funeral-home door, and motioned her over. We reentered the empty viewing room. I told her all we'd learned.

She said, "I can't believe I didn't know some of these things. I know these past couple years I've been learning less, but . . ." She shrugged. "Anyway, I didn't know. I did find out a tidbit about Denise Flowers. She was born in Buenos Aires. An American archeologist for a father, and an Argentinian mother. Supposedly a romantic beauty. It's probably not much help, but it's all I found out this evening. Want me to see what else I can find out?"

"Yes," I said. I thought a minute. "I wonder if Donna showed up tonight?"

"I'll check," Meg said.

She left the room but was back in less than a minute. "She just walked out."

Scott and I hurried to catch up with her.

Outside, a quick glance around showed no one in the parking lot. I listened for a car engine starting but heard nothing.

"Missed her," Scott said.

I leaned down to look through the windshields of the parked cars. I grabbed his arm. In the far corner of the parking lot, nearly hidden by the dangling limbs of a willow tree, I'd seen the dome light inside a car flash on and off. "It's Donna," I whispered. In the brief illumination, I'd caught a glimpse of her.

I listened for the start of the car. I debated dashing after her now or running to our car and chasing after her. Minutes of silence passed. I said, "Odd. I thought she'd start the car."

A car swung into the parking lot. I pulled Scott and myself into a shadow of the funeral parlor. I said, "Let's pay her a little visit."

Scott nodded. Crouching down, we skulked between cars until we stopped behind a gray station wagon, ten feet from Donna's car.

I inched my head up to get a glimpse into Donna's car. "She isn't alone," I said.

Scott raised his head. He nodded in confirmation. "You recognize who it is?"

I looked again. Their heads were close together in earnest conversation. They weren't interested in us. I glanced at the entrance to the funeral parlor. We were well hidden. Only the owner of the station wagon would see us if he or she came to get the car.

On hands and knees I crawled to my left. I felt the cool asphalt and tiny stones on my palms and through my pants. I hoped I wouldn't rip them. Next to the front tire, I paused and lifted my head. The passenger door of Donna's BMW opened. The two heads leaned together. I watched a lingering passionate kiss. They separated. An arm and a leg, quickly followed by a slender torso topped with permed hair: Bluefield. They whispered good nights. Bluefield fled into the darkness. I hurried forward, yanked open the passenger door, and jumped in.

Donna said, "What the hell?"

I looked back. Scott hurried forward. I unlocked the back door. He joined us.

Dalrymple stared at us angrily.

I said, "You're having sexual relations with Dan Bluefield?"

In a swift motion, she grabbed her purse and swung it at me. Before it slammed into the side of my head, I caught it and held it tight.

"I just saw that with Bluefield," I said. "It wasn't an innocent kiss. You've been bullheaded and unreasonable about Bluefield, and we're getting to the bottom of this whole problem. You should be supporting your fellow teachers and helping them out, not screwing some sixteen-year-old."

"He's eighteen," she said.

I eased my grip on her purse. "You *have* been having sex with him."

"I didn't say that," Dalrymple said.

"You didn't have to," I said. I stared directly into her eyes. "Tell me no, lie to me if you dare. We have other sources that confirm it, besides the obvious we've seen here."

She reached in her purse, came out with a pack of Virginia Slims, rolled down her window, lit a cigarette, and blew a long plume of smoke into the night air. "What is this, the Inquisition?" she said. "You have no right to interrogate me."

"How did Jones find out?" I asked.

Dalrymple looked stubborn and uncooperative.

I said, "If you don't talk, I'm going right to Carolyn Blackburn with this. And don't think we won't get the truth. If some kid's had sex with an adult, he's bragged to his friends. Some teenager will blab."

Dalrymple's shoulder slumped. She exhaled another stream of cigarette smoke. "I'm not sure how Jones found out. I think Dan may have told one of his friends who got in trouble. Dan swore he hadn't told anyone, but I think one of his buddies traded the information for leniency from Jones. Whatever way he found out, he came to me with the information early last week."

"Why have sex with a kid?" Scott asked.

"Because . . . because . . ." She snuffed the cigarette out in the ashtray. "Because he was kind and warm and my husband ignores me. It made Dan feel good, and me, too. On the days we had sex he would always calm down. He'd be better, more cooperative. I enjoyed it," she finished defiantly.

"How long's this been going on?" I asked.

"Is it important? I'm not going to give you dates, times, and his cock size. I'm going to have to quit anyway. Jones was actually fairly calm about it. I've been expecting Carolyn Blackburn to visit me anytime. Maybe Jones was true to his word and didn't tell anybody. He'd be the first administrator I know who was."

"He threatened to tell?" I asked.

"Oh, yes. To bring me up in front of the school board and everything. I couldn't take the public humiliation. My husband would divorce me. I probably wouldn't go to jail. Society in its infinite hypocrisy doesn't frown quite so hard on women who seduce eighteen-year-olds."

We sat in silence. She had smoked half of another cigarette before I said, "I don't want to bring harm to you. I just want to find out who killed Jones. You've got a motive. Do you know of anybody else?"

She gave me a disgusted look, ground out the burning

ash and said, "This is only a rumor. Jones was after Denise Flowers's teaching job. She thought he was going to try and fire her. I'm not sure how much was her own paranoia, and how much was real. I know this is only her second year teaching, and she wasn't tenured yet."

One of the innovations Jones had started was to take the evaluation of all nontenured teachers out of the hands of the heads of departments. This had caused a major uproar, but he'd gotten his way. By evaluating the new teachers himself, he thought to build a corps of good young teachers.

Minutes later we watched her drive away.

"I feel sorry for her," Scott said.

"She's got a motive for murder," I said, then sighed. "She didn't give us much to go on."

"But it's worth checking out," Scott said, then added: "You know in some ways this Jones guy doesn't seem to be so awful. He had some pretty powerful stuff on some of these people. He could have simply blown the whistle and ruined some careers. At least he gave them a chance to save their reputations."

"I'm not sure they all saw it like that," I said.

"Well, some of these cases are pretty complex. I'm not sure what I'd do if I had somebody's career or reputation in my hands. He had to make some tough decisions. All these teachers had reason to fear him. They'd all done something that, if it got out, would ruin their reputations."

I said, "A lot of them were in trouble because Jones was a vigilant, competent administrator. His own competence killed him."

"Yeah," Scott said, "but it was also his method of being kind. He gave all these people a chance to save their skins. Somebody tried to off him before he could tell. It was his promise of discretion, his kindness that killed him."

I agreed. We decided to stick around the wake for a while trying to see if Denise Flowers showed up. We reentered the funeral parlor and for the next hour we stayed in the background observing. By checking the sign-in book I found she hadn't been there, but my cursory look showed over half the faculty had been in so far that afternoon and evening to pay their respects.

While we waited we filled Meg in on the latest. She waited with us for a while, but left after half an hour saying she had to get home.

We thought about leaving, too. It was nearly ten, and the crowd had thinned out considerably. I saw Carolyn Blackburn walk in the door. She spotted us and came right over. She nodded at Scott and said to me, "I've got to talk to you."

We returned to the empty parlor.

Carolyn said, "We just got done with the school-board meeting. We couldn't call it off on such short notice. We were just going to do a memorial to Jones and adjourn, but Mr. Bluefield showed up."

I got an uneasy feeling. "This doesn't sound good," I said.

Carolyn said, "He demanded to make a public statement. They can't refuse him, because they've got that public-comment part of the meeting. He mentioned your name in the first sentence, Tom. I immediately stepped in and said that any comments about teachers had to be made in closed session. The board president immediately called for an executive session. Before we let Bluefield in, I told the board they better be careful. We had to protect your rights, Tom, and the board had to cover its ass."

"You let Bluefield in to talk to the board!" I was furious. "You let that bigoted, ignorant fool address the school board? All he had to do was show up, and he gets an audience. This lunatic shows up, and he gets to say anything he wants?"

Scott said, "Carolyn is trying to help, Tom. She's on your side."

She said to Scott, "Tom has a right to be angry. If I'd known Bluefield was coming, I could have taken more vigorous action, but he surprised us all."

I shook my head. "I can't believe this," I said. "How dare

the board give in to this maniac? This isn't the first time he's caused trouble. You all should have known he was an idiot. By letting him talk to the board, you've encouraged him."

"He didn't get his way, Tom. You will not be fired. Not as long as I have any say in the matter, and you know you have legal protections."

"Is this about Tom's being gay?" Scott asked.

"No, although Bluefield tried to bring that up. I was fairly proud of the school-board president"—this was Jessica Allen, recently elected—"she stopped him each time he tried to mention you. She made him talk about his kid. Still, Bluefield managed to get in a few licks."

I found that I was sitting in the chair Younger had sat in while we questioned him. Carolyn walked over and sat next to me. "Don't be angry. We stopped him. Kept him busy enough so he couldn't get out to make any statements to the press. First thing tomorrow I'm going to call the reporters for the two River's Edge papers. They owe me a couple of favors. I'll do everything I can to keep anything Bluefield ever might say out of the papers. I think I'll be successful."

I mumbled thanks. She left.

Scott came over and sat next to me. He put his hand on my shoulder and squeezed it. He said softly, "Let's go home."

In the car I said, "I need to stop at my place for a couple of things first."

"We've got enough stuff at my place." This was true. We're close enough in size so that we can wear each other's clothes, but I insisted that I needed a few essentials.

As we crossed 191st Street at Wolf Road on the way to my place, several emergency vehicles passed us, sirens blaring. I had my arm out the window, my head resting all the way back in the seat cushions.

As we pulled over to let the fire truck pass, I sniffed the

pleasant autumn air. It contained barely a hint of the cold of winter lurking only a month or so away.

Up the rise and over Interstate 80 and I saw the flashing lights of the emergency vehicles beyond the white oil-storage silos on the right.

I sat up straight. "What the hell?" I asked.

We drew closer. They were at my place. Looking through the trees, I could see fire streaming out the bedroom and kitchen windows. A fireman tried to wave us past, but we pulled into the driveway. He cursed and swore and came up to the driver's side of the car. I leaped from the car, not pausing or caring what Scott said to him. I raced to the house like some idiot in a cheap movie. I heard shouts around me, then felt arms encircling me and drawing me back.

I watched my home burn to ashes.

6

I remember bits and pieces of the next few hours. I know Scott stood next to me, his closeness providing comfort. A couple of firemen eventually recognized him and tried to come over and talk, but he waved them away. Somebody handed us coffee and sandwiches. I only took a couple of bites before throwing mine away.

Finally the last fire truck sat at the top of the driveway, ten feet from the damp and blackened embers. I found myself sitting next to Scott in the front seat of his car.

"It's three in the morning," Scott said. "We should go. There's nothing you can do here." His voice was its softest and most soothing.

"In a few minutes," I said. I got out of the car and walked to the place that had been my home for fifteen years. The smell of smoke and ash permeated the air. Under my feet the ground had been turned to mud by the water the firemen poured in their vain attempt to stem the flames.

A fireman met me a few feet from the house. He was a roly-poly man about twenty-five years old. "Mr. Mason," he said, "there's nothing you can do here now. It's still too dangerous for you to go in. We're going to stay here a while longer. We think it's out, but we always like to be sure. There'll be an arson investigation in the morning."

"Was it arson?" I asked.

He looked doubtful. "I'm not the expert," he said, "but it sure was caught good when we got here."

"Arson," I said.

I began to walk around the house.

The fireman said, "Here, Mr. Mason, I wish you wouldn't. I could get in trouble if you hurt yourself."

"I promise not to go next to the house. I just want to walk around."

I noticed Scott was beside me. He accompanied me as I took the most painful journey of my life. Opposite where the back door used to be, I stopped. I said, "You know what I'll miss the most?"

"What?" Scott asked quietly.

"The first gift you gave me. I've saved it all these years. You bought it back from Japan that first October. You remember that silk rose? It was unique. They only make them like that over there. It was so beautiful. Now it's gone."

Scott said what needed to be said: "Be thankful we weren't in there. We're alive. That's what counts. And you've got a place to stay."

I glanced at him in the darkness of the now-cool night. "I know that's true." I sighed. "I don't care about the expensive stuff. It's the irreplaceable stuff. Pictures of us together on vacations, family stuff." I was too tired and in too much shock to cry. "If it was arson . . ." I began.

Scott interrupted, "If it was arson, we'll find the person and make them sorry."

"If it was arson," I said, "I know who it was. Dan Bluefield."

In the car on the way to the city, I raged about Dan Bluefield. How Scott kept silent so long, I'll never know. He didn't tell me to shut up or to give it a rest. He let me fulminate all the way to where we exited Lake Shore Drive at LaSalle Street. I finally wound down as we left the Drive.

I sat in the penthouse library, surrounded on three sides by the floor-to-ceiling bookcases. The fourth wall consisted of windows looking north toward Lincoln Park. I didn't turn on any of the lights, but stared out at the darkness. Scott's building is the tallest around, so the view to the rest of the world is never obstructed.

He came into the room in jeans and socks. He touched my hand lightly. "Do you want to try to get some sleep?" he asked.

"It's okay," I said. "I won't be able to sleep anyway. I'll just sit here. Maybe I'll try to read something later."

He patted my shoulder and said good night.

After he left, I walked to the window. For a long time I stared out, watching the cars move far below. Around five-thirty I tried to find something to read to blank out my mind. I placed a Jean Redpath CD into the machine, hoping her soft Scottish burr might help soothe me to sleep. Every time I thought I might be nodding off, the vision of the flames leaping out my bedroom window flashed through my mind. The words on the pages held no sense for me. I thought about the items I'd miss. The other gifts from Scott: a stuffed Eeyore from our first Christmas, a pewter *Lord of the Rings* chess set, the scroll of a love poem he'd written for our tenth anniversary, the dowdy throw pillow we brought in the South of France. The pillow had our names hand-embroidered, along with obscene comments in French about lovemaking between two men. Most of the stuff was not very expensive, just irreplaceable. I watched the light of the rising sun slowly spread over the city scape below.

It was Saturday, so there was no school. I wouldn't have gone anyway.

At eight I found a diet soda in the refrigerator in the kitchen and then I looked in on Scott. He slept peacefully on his stomach. I gazed at his broad shoulders, uncovered by the blanket, then traced the line of his still-covered torso, down the sensuous curves of his thighs and hips, down his long muscular legs.

I let him sleep. I returned to the library, sipped the diet soda, and curled up with a volume of Wordsworth's collected poems, guaranteed at any normal time to put me to sleep in less than five minutes. At some point Wordsworth must have worked his magic, because I came wide awake at the ringing of the phone. I glanced at the clock on the dark oak desk. It was just after nine-thirty. My head felt numb and my body ached from sleeping in the chair. I snatched the phone off the stand on the third ring.

It was Hank Daniels from the River's Edge police. He offered condolences, then said, "I got in earlier, saw the report on the night log. I went out to the fire scene, just got back. It was arson. You need to come in so we can talk."

As I was finishing my conversation, Scott walked in, dressed only in jockey shorts. "Who was it?" he asked after I hung up.

I told him. He looked at the clock. "Did you get any sleep?"

"About an hour."

"You're in no condition to go running around town. You need to get some rest, relax. It's going to be hard enough to go back there and check for anything you can salvage, although I don't guess there'll be much."

"Let me take a shower," I said. "I'll be ready to go. Somebody burned my home, and I'm going to make them pay." I felt last night's anger returning, only now it wasn't fury, it was cold determination to find and punish the perpetrator.

Scott insisted we stop for breakfast first. We ate thick French toast at Nookies on Wells Street; then we went out to River's Edge.

We stopped at the police station. With the trees in full color around it, the old place almost looked respectable. In the starkness of winter it would be revealed for what it was, a run-down rat trap. Daniels and Johnson met us at the front desk and took us to a gray interrogation room.

"Do you think this is connected to the murder?" Scott asked.

Daniels said, "Cops have an instinct that says never believe in coincidences. This is too much of one. We know

102

you've been talking to people on the faculty about the murder. We want to know what you found out."

For half an hour they barraged us with questions. I was too tired and angry to be reasonable. Often I felt my temper rise, especially when at one point they seemed to be implying that we might have set the fire ourselves, but Scott's calm managed to remind me to take it easy.

Finally I said, "I'm the one who's had his house burned down. You said it was arson. I'm the victim. I refuse to be treated as if I'm guilty. Let's get my lawyer in here, and we can all have a nice chat."

Daniels said, "We're simply asking the standard questions we would in any arson investigation."

I was only slightly mollified by that statement. I wished Frank Murphy was back from vacation.

Daniels continued, "What you've done since the murder, and we know you've been questioning people, may have angered somebody with a guilty secret. Whoever set the fire may have thought you were at home. Your truck, Mr. Mason, was in full view back by the barn."

I used the old barn part-time as a garage. With so much harvesting equipment being used in the area, the farmer who owns the fields had asked me if he could store some of it in the barn. Fortunately the truck was far enough away from the house not to get caught in the conflagration of the night before.

"If it was Bluefield, he'd have only seen me driving that to school. He wouldn't have known about the Porsche," I said.

"Do you really think the kid did it?" Daniels asked.

"Yes, and I don't think it had anything to do with the murder. I think the kid is fucking nuts, and he'd do anything to hurt me. That's going to stop today."

"Don't do anything stupid," Daniels warned.

Before I could retort Scott asked, "Do they know how it started?"

Daniels said, "Once they started looking this morning, it didn't take long. Molotov cocktails through the windows, one in the bedroom, one in the kitchen. No other clues so far. With all the fire equipment around the place last night, they won't find any footprints or tire tracks. You don't have a lot of neighbors, but those few will be asked if they saw anything. I doubt if they did. With all the corn around your place still unharvested, it would have been difficult for anyone to see anything close to the house."

Daniels added, "Two things you might be interested to know. First, we went to the Bluefield house to question the kid about the arson. Second, we don't believe him about seeing you outside the principal's office."

"Thanks," I said.

"Don't misunderstand," Johnson said, "you're still our chief suspect."

Scott's hand on my arm forestalled a comment. He asked, "Did the kid have an alibi for last night?"

"He was at home, so he says, and his old man backs him up. Mr. Bluefield was quite self-righteous and self-satisfied about your home burning down. The kid didn't say a lot. We questioned him about the murder again. The kid's a jerk and would make a lousy witness."

"That doesn't sound like a ringing endorsement of my innocence," I said.

Sounding more reasonable than he had so far, Daniels said, "We've got to ask questions. It's not a polite job, and you *are* a good suspect. People have been convicted based on only one of the things you're accused of: last one to see victim alive, fights with victim the day he dies, finds the dead body, has blood on his shirt."

I began to list the arguments against these reasons.

Daniels held up a hand. "Save it. You aren't under arrest. Although you could be for obstructing justice. So far we haven't gotten any complaints about your interference. Nobody willing to press charges or say anything nasty, which is lucky for you. If these people are talking, they seem to trust you. Learning all that information can be dangerous. So can fucking with the cops, so don't try it. I'm

104

not Frank Murphy, and his word only goes so far around here, so I'd be careful, if I were you."

We said nothing to this, and a few minutes later they let us go.

We drove to my house. When Scott pulled up the driveway, the sight of the ruin by the light of day hit me hard. The investigation team was just about finished so I was allowed to prowl carefully through the ruins. The basement stairs had been destroyed. Little remained of the furniture. Globs of plastic were all that remained of the electronics room: computers, stereo, CD player. The place smelled as black and depressing as it looked.

Scott followed me silently. His calm presence got me through the inspection. I didn't find one salvageable thing. I stood in the middle of the blackened ruin and felt all the helplessness and powerlessness of the night before back again and redoubled, but those feelings had a companion this morning, a towering fury. I'd get whoever did this.

We had dirt and soot all over our clothes, so we went to the barn to change. We'd brought spare clothes with us, because we knew we'd be stopping at the house. When I finished dressing and reopened the door to look out on the field of corn surrounding the ruin, I said, "We're going to Bluefield's."

Scott said, "Fine."

I turned back to look at him. "I thought you'd object," I said.

"No," he said.

Usually Scott's the reasonable one in our relationship. The one who insists we stop, think, and consider all options. From ten years of knowing him I could tell that his "No" contained all the fury of someone ready to do battle. I mentioned earlier, he doesn't lose his temper often, but when he does it's spectacular. I didn't envy Dan Bluefield his chances when we caught up with him.

We stopped at school. There is rarely a day or time that some group isn't using the school during off hours. Everybody from the Cub Scouts to the Park District uses the complex for meetings or games. I needed to stop in the office to find Bluefield's address. We found Carolyn sitting at Jones's desk, and told her about the fire.

"This is too much," she said. She looked us over. "You're all right?"

We nodded.

"Could you save anything?"

I told her about our visit to the scene this morning.

"I'm sorry" was her response.

I asked carefully about the people we'd talked to so far. She gave no hint of knowing any of the secrets we'd uncovered. Jones had kept his promises to say nothing.

We left her at the principal's office, trying to do that job as well as her own. They'd have one of the assistants as a temporary replacement, but even she would need to be trained.

In the outer office I picked up the phone.

"Who are you calling?" Scott asked.

"Meg. I've got an idea about finding out where all our suspects were last night."

First I told Meg about the fire. She was instantly sympathetic and horrified, and then angry. She insisted we come over to her house. I assured her we were okay and told her we were going to question the Bluefields, but that we needed her help with something else. I barely got the suggestion started before she picked up on it.

"I'll do all the calls. Leave it to me. I've got the old grapevine going. I haven't been this involved in ages, but I'll find out where all of them were. I wasn't Gossip Central for years for nothing."

"Don't forget to be discreet," I reminded her.

"You must be really tired," she said, "to think that I need to be reminded about discretion. Trust me."

I did trust her, so I shut up.

We got Bluefield's address from my desk files, and drove over.

They lived in a modified Cape Cod on a cul-de-sac in the oldest part of River's Edge. The neighborhood had been

106

built before tract houses became the rage. They didn't have sidewalks, but drainage ditches along both sides of the road. The large spaces between the houses were remnants of the area's recent rural past. The home itself looked to have had several recent, expensive renovations.

We stormed up to the door, prepared to do battle. We knocked and pounded. Nobody answered. We walked around the house. No cars in the driveway. We peered through a small window into the garage. Empty. A dog in the house on the right barked at us as we walked back to the front. Standing on the lawn, we mulled over the possibilities: They had fled; we'd just missed them; they were hiding in the house. Since we were getting nowhere, I figured we might as well find out everything I could about the Bluefields.

A curtain moved in the house on the right, and a minute later a man emerged from inside. A large German shepherd accompanied him out the door. The house had two stories and was more than substantial. The man plodded through the leaves being dropped by the massive oaks throughout the neighborhood. He stood well over six foot six, with gray hair, and muscles still not gone to fat. He must have been in his mid-fifties.

He stopped when he got to us. Without a command that I could see, the dog immediately sat next to him on his left. "Looking for the Bluefields?" he asked.

We said yes. He stared at Scott. We got the recognition issue out of the way. Then the man said, "They took off together. The old man and the boy, about seven this morning. Mrs. Bluefield left about fifteen, maybe twenty minutes ago."

"Any idea where they went?" I asked.

"Nope. The boy in some kind of trouble again? I'd heard he'd reformed. Haven't had any trouble with him myself for quite a while."

"We just want to question him," I said. "I'm his English teacher."

"He still goes to school? I'm a little surprised at that.

'Course you're not the first teacher, social worker, administrator, or cop to come over trying to talk to him. That family's had a parade of folks through here over the years. Ask me, all the kid needs is a new set of parents and a swift kick in the rear."

"You must know a lot," Scott said.

He invited us into his home for coffee. We sat in the kitchen, a built-in microwave attesting to its modernity. He ground the coffee himself. The aroma was wonderful, and the coffee delicious. We talked baseball for a while before returning to the subject of the neighbors. The dog sat next to his master's chair, head on paws, as if listening to our whole conversation.

The man told us he didn't want us to think he was a busybody, but he'd been a neighbor of the Bluefields since he moved into the neighborhood five years ago. "Trouble. That's the one word that sums them up the best. Father's an unreconstructed hippie. Sells drugs out of the house, I'm sure."

"Police know about that?" I asked.

"Hell, yes. They've come to get the dad a couple times. I think he served a few months in prison a couple years back."

"How about the mother?" Scott asked.

"The cops took her a few times. If the mister isn't home, she takes care of the customers. I don't think she's ever actually been arrested, at least not while I've lived here."

"You had any trouble with them?" I asked.

He laughed, then said, "Who hasn't? Talk to everybody. They'll have horror stories to tell. My time came about a month after I moved in here. One night my electricity failed. I figured it was a blackout, but I looked outside and everybody else's lights were still on. I thought that was odd, so I went outside to check the circuit breakers in the garage. Out in the darkness I heard shouts of 'Wimp,' 'Jerk,' 'Fool,' other idiotic shit. I found a window broken in the side door of the garage. They'd gotten in and turned off all the circuits. I looked around, but whoever it was ran off.

Next day I replaced the glass, vowing to be more vigilant, maybe look into a security system. Although one of the reasons I moved out here was to avoid that kind of thing. I was plenty pissed."

He drained his coffee cup, refilled it, and offered us more. "Same damn thing happened the next night. I stuck my head out the back door, and the name-calling continued. I came back in and called the police." He hunched himself closer to the table and smiled. "I enjoy this next part," he said. "With all the lights out whoever it was couldn't see me sneak out the front door. I'd heard the direction the shouts came from. I walked around the block and came up through the backyards. I wound up ten feet behind two kids. The cop car pulled up my driveway with the siren off, but with the lights flashing. The kids backed right up into me. I grabbed them both. One managed to squirm away. I held onto the other one. It was little Dan Bluefield, thirteen years old."

"What did you do?" Scott asked.

"I'm an ex-cop. Worked the Twelfth District in Chicago, one of the toughest in the city. I yanked the shit out of the little bastard. I know a few tricks about hurting someone without leaving scars or bruises. Almost pulled the kid's hair out by the roots. I had the boy in tears almost before I started. He cried and blubbered. I told him if anything ever happened to my home, I'd blame him and come looking for him. Never had any trouble since then."

"Why not set the dog on him?" I asked.

"Didn't have Fido then. Got him a few weeks later. They retired him from police work. He got hurt pretty bad in his last bust. They were going to destroy him, but with the help of a good vet, I nursed him back to health. I'm sure that over the years he's helped convince the kid to back off."

We left a few minutes later. As we contemplated which houses to go to next to ask questions, Scott asked, "Fido? He named his dog Fido?"

"Guy that big can name his dog Almathusta Gertrude

Gahagen if he wants to. Nobody's going to argue with him or the dog. Besides, somebody's got to name their dog Fido."

We tried the tan brick ranch house to the left of the Bluefields'. A couple in their late twenties talked to us in their living room. We did the obligatory baseball chat. They hadn't seen the Bluefields this morning. They repeated the stories about police visits and drugs.

The woman said, "Sometimes the buyers just drive up in their cars and toot their horns. Whoever's home—Mom, Dad, the kid—runs out and takes care of business."

"And the police do nothing?" Scott asked.

They shrugged. She said, "We reported them once. The police came, saw nothing happening, took our names, talked to the Bluefields, and arrested nobody."

He said, "That's when we started having trouble. We found garbage, food, all over our front porch. This happened several times over a period of four weeks. We called the police once. We told them we suspected the Bluefields. The police talked to them. We kept watch the next few nights, but even alternating watches, we lost too much sleep. We both have jobs. The second time we didn't keep watch, we woke to find garbage all over the front lawn."

She said, "It was terrible. It took over a day to clean it up. I felt that awful Mr. Bluefield watching me all day long. His son came out and stood a step off our property for over an hour. He didn't say anything. Just stared and sneered. It scared me."

"We didn't call the police after that. Eventually it stopped. We thought about moving, but we just can't. We could barely afford the down payment on this place."

Next we tried the neighbors on the street directly behind the Bluefields. This turned out to be an older couple, probably in their seventies. The woman had grown up in the house, then come back to live in it after her parents died. Introducing ourselves did not cause a spate of baseball recognition. They weren't fans. It was refreshing.

They, too, had their trouble with the notorious Bluefields. Living behind them, they'd missed a lot of the drug-selling that went on out front.

"Spray paint," the woman told us. "We're Jewish. For years we had no trouble. Our kids grew up. We gave them a good Jewish upbringing. Everything was fine, just like you'd expect it to be in America. Then it started. Swastikas on the garage door. Cruel things on the sides of the house. The police were kind, but couldn't do anything. We tried watching, ourselves."

He said, "We talked to some friends who had some trouble at one of the synagogues up in Chicago. I guess I can tell you this." He looked to his wife for confirmation. She nodded her head yes.

"They sent some people out to watch for us. People who knew how to watch. They sent us on vacation. When we came back, our garage was totally repainted. We suspected there'd been trouble. The leader of the group reported to us. They'd repainted the garage. They'd also caught who did it: the Bluefields. They told us they didn't think there'd ever be trouble again, but if there was, to call them. We asked if we should call the police. I remember the man smiled at me and said we could if we wanted, but he didn't think it would help."

The woman smiled broadly and said, "We didn't ask any more, and there hasn't been any trouble since. If we ever see the Bluefield boy at the local store or anywhere around town, he goes out of his way to be polite to us."

No one answered in the first two houses across the street from the Bluefields. So far people had horror stories to tell, but couldn't give us a clue to where the Bluefields were, or when they might be back.

The third house across the street, this one a red-brick ranch, had a different story. When she found out what we wanted, the woman, who was in her early forties, swept us into the house. She had long red fingernails, carefully tended, and wore a Chicago Bulls warmup outfit, right down to a pair of Air Jordans. She sat down and talked with very little prodding from us.

"That boy dated my daughter last year. I didn't say anything. You know how contrary kids can be at that age. Tell them yes and they want no, or vice versa. Makes no difference. If Mom likes it, it's got to be awful. So I kept my mouth shut. My girl went through hell. I watched as carefully as I could. I knew the stories about drugs over there. Sheer chance that she took a camping trip with some friends and met a nice boy from Mokena. She broke up with Dan Bluefield. He started harassing her. We called the police. We started getting obscene phone calls. We got a tap in here, but you know the phone company will only put one in for two weeks."

I hadn't known that.

"The fifteenth day, the calls started again. I went nuts with the phone company. They put on another tap. Of course, you know what happened. Day fifteen, they started again. Then I guess Julie, that's my daughter, told her boyfriend. He's on the football team at Lincoln-Way High School. Julie wouldn't tell me the whole story, but from what she said I guess her new boyfriend got some of his buddies, and they paid Dan a visit. The calls stopped after that."

She didn't know where Dan or the parents might be.

"Would Julie know?" I asked.

"She won't be back until late this afternoon. You're welcome to come back then and ask her."

We thanked her and told her we'd drop by later.

We stopped for lunch at the McDonald's on LaGrange Road in Frankfort. It was two-thirty, so the place was uncrowded. One fan asked for an autograph. None of the teenaged servers recognized Scott. When you pitch two no-hitters in the World Series and bring a baseball championship to Chicago for the first time in decades, it's an oddity when you aren't recognized.

It took us three minutes to drive to Meg's in Frankfort. She lives in one of the beautiful Victorian homes in the old section of town.

She fussed over us, concerned about how we were coping with the aftermath of the fire. I told her I was concentrating my emotions on investigating the Bluefields, and that apart from being tired from lack of sleep I was okay. We sat in her living room, which was done in blue, the couch and love seat a deep navy with minute stars grouped in rectangles, the rug a light blue tending to turquoise. There was one large framed print of a sailing ship on each wall.

We told Meg about talking to the Bluefields' neighbors. She said, "I'm not surprised about what you found. A totally dysfunctional family." Then she added, "I've got the information on where everybody was."

"That quick?" I asked.

She patted my hand. "My dear, used to be half the time I knew things before people even did them. The old gossip-gathering skills aren't that rusty."

I smiled at her. She went on: "We've got everybody present and accounted for. Everybody has a solid alibi. None of the murder suspects could have set the fire."

"Except the Bluefield kid," Scott said.

"I couldn't find out anything about any of the Bluefields," Meg said.

Scott said, "A couple of the neighbors, and the girl Julie's boyfriend and his buddies, managed to successfully scare Bluefield. Now he's graduated to attacks like those on Tom."

"He's maturing," Meg said. "Maybe his next level is full-time drug dealer or hit man. Who knows?" Then she added, "Kurt Campbell and I have been doing some checking together, trying to find out if anybody besides the teachers you've talked to had problems with Jones."

I'd been concerned about the possibility of a teacher whose difficulties with Jones we didn't know about, or even someone totally unrelated to who and what we'd found so far, having simply showed up at school, killed Jones, and left undetected.

"We couldn't think of one, or find one. We did some

pretty extensive and very discreet checking. Of course, Kurt would know most of the problems anyway."

I thanked her for the help. We stayed until it was time for us to go back to talk to Dan Bluefield's ex-girlfriend.

We drove slowly past the Bluefields'. It was nearly six and beginning to get dark. No cars in the driveway and no lights on in the house.

We pulled up to the girlfriend's. She met us at the door. Hair cut short, she wore jeans and a pale orange sweatshirt. Her mother joined us in the living room. The seventeen-year-old took a while to get over the fact that Scott Carpenter was sitting in her living room. I didn't recognize her from school, which isn't unusual in a school with over three thousand kids.

We explained what we needed to know.

She looked thoughtful, tucked a leg under her, and then said, "I dated that creep for three months. I don't know what I saw in him. He was hateful so much of the time." She shuddered. "Then I met Darren." She gave us much the same version of the breakup with Bluefield and subsequent harassment as the mother had.

"Where could he be right now?" I asked.

"A couple places he hangs out with friends."

I asked if she could give us the names and addresses. She did so with alacrity. "I hope you make the creep miserable," she said as she wrote them down.

At the door while we were leaving she said, "If you try those and he's not there, you might try the forest preserve on Route 30 just east of Wolf Road. Him and his buddies sometimes got together there to hang out, drink beer, and harass people."

We thanked her and left. The addresses she gave us were in Frankfort Square, Tinley Park, Orland Park, and Mokena. We struck out at all of them.

"Want to try the forest preserve?" Scott asked.

"Why not? Although I think it closes at dusk." It was nearly eight and full dark.

At the entrance to the park a chain barred our way. Scott

114

turned the Porsche around, prepared to leave, but I caught a light among the trees. "Somebody's there," I said.

He let the car idle and looked back. "Where?" he said. "I don't see anything."

I pointed.

"I don't see anything," he repeated.

He began to turn back, but I said, "Wait." We both stared for a few minutes, then it came again.

"Glow of a cigarette being puffed," I said. "Never forget how that looks in the dark, not after being in the Marines. Let's investigate."

Scott said, "There can't be any cars in there. The chain's on. Or if there is somebody, it's got to be official people who have a right to be there."

"It's our last lead," I said. I opened the door and got out.

"Will you wait?" he asked. "I'm going to move the car away from the entrance. I don't want the police coming in and investigating what the hell *we're* doing here." He drove the car about thirty feet down the road and parked it behind a screen of trees.

The area of the forest preserve closest to the road was mostly open field, with picnic tables interspersed around outdoor grills. We crossed this quickly. Lights from the cars passing by on Route 30 lit the way enough to the edge of the trees so we didn't trip over ourselves. As we entered the woods and got deeper inside, we moved more carefully. Leaves rustled underfoot. A light breeze had sprung up, carrying a stray leaf or two with it. The perfect autumn weather held.

We found a road that wound through the woods, and tied to stay on its edge. This way we avoided rustling leaves with our passage, but could leap into the foliage if someone came along. Taking the road made the search longer, since it wasn't a direct route toward the light we'd seen.

Finally we spotted a car in the distance, but no lights around it.

"Careful," I whispered to Scott.

115

We crept up on it quietly. Ten feet from the rear bumper, I said, "I don't think there's anybody in it." We made it all the way to the back fender without arousing any suspicion or seeing anyone. Up close a rack of lights on the top gave us the news.

Scott found it necessary to say, "It's a cop car."

I rested a hand on the fender and peered into the darkness surrounding us. "What's it doing here?" I asked.

"Sitting parked," he said. I love him dearly, but there are times the man could use a good whap upside the head.

I inched around to the side door and raised my head slowly until I could see inside. It was empty.

I returned to him and reported its uninhabited state.

He whispered, "Then let's get the hell out of here before the cop returns."

Suddenly a light flashed in the distance on the right side of the road. We heard a giggle. The light stayed on. We could make out a path toward where the light shone. We moved slowly along the dirt, fortunately a well-used way, with few leaves. After a few yards we saw a clearing and two people. A man and a woman, both mostly naked. We saw him fumbling in the light in his discarded pants. He murmured, "I know I have a condom in here somewhere." We heard a sigh of satisfaction, and he reached over and snapped off the flashlight. In the darkness I saw a tiny ember of ash nestled in a hollow of dirt. We waited several giggles' worth and backed away.

"Well, Sherlock," Scott said as we strode carefully farther down the asphalt drive, "your ability to track the evildoers seems to be a little rusty."

I whispered back, "Light of my life, angel of my existence, true love forever: Shut the fuck up."

He had the nerve to chuckle.

We proceeded in silence for fifteen minutes. Finally he said, "I think the path is doubling back toward the entrance. It must make a complete circle. Only those two lovebirds are here."

I grabbed his arm. "There." I pointed to a spot in the distance.

He hesitated. "It's just them again," he said.

"No car on the road," I said. "It's somebody else. This is a wavering light, not a steady one from a flashlight. But it's not from a cigarette either."

We found no path this time, so our progress through the leaves was slower. As we neared our goal, we heard raucous voices with a background of the thump of softly played rock music. They kept no watch, obviously feeling that they were alone. Fortunately, they were loud enough so that the leaves we disturbed didn't arouse any suspicion. We inched our way forward and crouched behind a tree at the edge of the light.

Up close we could observe the group. The light came from two candles sitting on top of a boom box. I also saw the glow of two cigarette butts, cupped in sheltering hands. I quickly corrected that observation when both butts were passed around: pot. I counted six people. They talked and laughed unconcernedly. Being observed or caught seemed the furthest thing from their minds. Three sat on a blanket on the ground; the others perched on top of a picnic table. The one closest to me on the table was maybe ten feet away. I saw him in profile. Razor-thin, with his hair permed. Had to be Dan Bluefield. This was confirmed a minute later when he said, "This is great stuff. The new shipment we got in today is the best we've gotten in a while."

A female voice I didn't recognize issued from one of the people on the ground.

"Your dad is so cool. I wish mine was like that. Getting drugs any time you want."

Bluefield gave a contented laugh.

Another voice, this one male, said, "I think it's even better the way he came to school to try and get that faggot Mason fired. It's so great when your dad backs you up against those stupid teachers."

"Don't say faggot," a third voice said.

117

He got hooted and sneered at and called several names. He defended himself by saying, "Lay off. My uncle's gay. He's cool. You shouldn't talk that way."

The rest spent several minutes belittling the concept of tolerance.

The first female voice switched the topic slightly when she said, "Did you guys hear about Mason's house burning?"

"The faggot got what he deserved," Bluefield said. "You should have seen what I did to him yesterday." The teenager explained in vivid detail about depositing the dead rat and other debris on my desk. He got a few squeals of "Yuck!" amid the general sounds of approval.

As I listened to his casual explanation and mocking laughter, I felt horrific anger building inside me.

They discussed the fire. The conclusion they came to was, Too bad I didn't die in the fire too.

"The hope of America," Scott murmured.

He spoke softly and next to my ear, but the six teenagers were immediately silent.

"What was that?" one said.

"Quiet," another said.

Someone blew out the candles. The radio clicked off.

It was difficult to see in the dimness, but I thought one of the figures moved toward where we were hidden. I reached back for Scott and found he wasn't there. I hadn't heard him move. Suddenly his voice rang out from ten feet to my left. "Everybody freeze." His deep voice rang with the authority of any television cop. The teenagers only hesitated a second. Bluefield yelled, "Run!" A figure came right toward me. As it ran past, I reached out from my hiding place and grabbed.

The person struggled fiercely. I felt a cast on one arm. Bluefield. My anger flared. I slammed the body against the ground. Moments later I heard footsteps close by. Scott said, "Tom?"

"I think I've got Bluefield," I said between gasps.

The kid heard our voices and his struggles redoubled.

He got the arm with the cast on it loose for a second and swung it at me. I caught it and began to twist. He squealed in pain, and stopped struggling.

I listened carefully. No sound of the others. None of them had stayed to see the aftermath. A minute later we heard the sound of a truck or van starting.

I said, "There go your buddies."

Bluefield snarled at me. Scott held the kid while I made my way to the picnic table, stumbling only once in the dimness. I felt the surface of the table. I knocked something over, patted the tabletop, and picked up an object. Seconds later a wavering flame from a cigarette lighter lit the area. I swung it around to get a view of the clearing.

Scott brought the kid to the table. As soon as he got close enough, Bluefield kicked out at me. I caught his leg and twisted it. He gave a yelp and stopped struggling.

"What if he tried to call for help?" Scott asked.

"Fine. It would be great to have the cops show up. He'll be nice and quiet. His friends are gone."

I found a plastic bag filled with marijuana on the ground nearby. I looked at Bluefield and said, "Tell me about the new shipment."

"Fuck you," Bluefield said.

"I think it's time for a manners lesson," I said. "Let's sit him down."

The kid struggled, and I was hampered by my cut arm, but eventually we jammed his ass onto the bench. We secured him to the table with our belts, then sat on either side of him.

"What are you going to do? Molest me?" he asked.

"Nothing that simple," I said.

Bluefield jerked his head in Scott's direction. "Gonna let your boyfriend do it? Aren't you man enough?"

I looked over at Scott. I'd relit the candles. The flickering light certainly wasn't enough to allow Bluefield to recognize Scott, although at this moment that wasn't a major concern.

Scott said, "If you don't shut up, I'm going to shove your head so far up your ass, you'll be spitting shit."

Bluefield said, "Fuck you," and spat in Scott's face.

An instant later Bluefield bent over, spitting blood or teeth onto the ground. I'm not sure I saw Scott's fist move. I did see him blowing on his knuckles.

I grabbed a handful of Bluefield's curls and yanked his head back. The light was good enough for me to see blood issuing from both a split lip and his nose.

"You don't get it yet, Bluefield," I said. "See, the faggots have captured you, and there are no witnesses. We can do anything we want. We can make it hurt, and we can make you suffer just as much as we want. I'd bet any money your friends won't come back. So it's just us, and you're like all bullies: When you're confronted, your true coward nature oozes from every pore."

His defiance at this point passed the realm of stupidity: He spat in *my* face. I didn't move, and this time I saw Scott's fist. That was because it took the kid a second to turn away from me. Once again he bent over, spitting debris from his mouth.

Again I yanked him up by his curls. I said, "They taught us a few things in the service. I got caught by the Viet Cong once. Learned a few interesting things from them before I escaped. I think we should try a few of those on you to-night."

7

Casually I reached behind me for one of the candles. I held the flame an inch from Bluefield's chin and saw fear in the kid's eyes. That made me feel good.

Bluefield gulped. "You wouldn't . . . torture me?"

Scott grabbed a mass of curls and yanked the head back and forth, then pulled the kid's face an inch from his own. "You've bullied enough people, and we're here in a perfect spot to get revenge for every single one of them."

I'd never heard the tone Scott used. Anger and towering hatred.

I put the candle down, got up, and paced in front of the two of them. "Let's see if we can't get a little information," I said. "Maybe he'll tell us enough. If he's real cooperative, we could let him go."

I picked up the candle again and held it near Bluefield's face. I saw fear and maybe anger in it, but I detected defiance underneath. Threats and intimidation from his neighbors and their protectors might have worked in junior high, but the kid was older and tougher now.

"Tell us about the drug shipment," I said, putting the candle back on the table.

Bluefield swore, then spat at me.

Scott's fist flicked out. Blood spurted from Bluefield's nose. Scott grabbed the kid's curls, yanked his head back, and twisted the fistful of hair until tears streamed down Bluefield's cheeks.

The kid moaned in agony. "Please, stop," he whispered.

Scott placed his lips an inch from Bluefield's ear. "You've fucked around with your last victim, you scummy little coward." Scott's tone even had me a little scared. "We're faggots and we're going to get revenge."

Bluefield began to cry. Scott stared at the eighteen-year-old for a minute, then stood up and walked to the edge of the light. He kept his back to us. I could see him trembling.

I turned back to Bluefield. He sobbed uncontrollably eventually mixing words with his blubbering. "Don't hurt me," he repeated over and over. At one point he choked on his own tears and snot, coughing violently. It took nearly ten minutes for him to get himself under control. I left him to pull himself together. I walked over to Scott. I murmured, "You okay?"

He shrugged his shoulders slightly and moved out of the light to the edge of the clearing, where he sat with his back against a tree. Moonlight shone on the right side of his face. I saw the glitter of tears.

I turned back to Bluefield. Except for an occasional sniffle, he had himself under control. Taking out my hanky, I sat next to him and wiped snot, tears, and blood from his face. I didn't untie him. I wasn't taking any chances. I held the hanky so he could blow his nose.

Several minutes and a few sniffles later I said, "Dan, I need you to tell me all about the drugs."

And he did. Today he and his dad had gone to their distributor in Chicago with a couple of friends. Dan had left with a buddy while his dad stayed in the city. They'd come out here to party. They knew of a little-used, unchained entrance to the forest preserve. It was only a dirt road and not kept in repair, but that made it all the better for teenagers, since discovery was highly unlikely. He told me about the drug operation, adding details about the dealing at school, about how deliveries were made, about where the stash was hidden in the house so the police could never find it when they searched.

When he finished he drew a deep breath and looked at me and said, "I'm really messed up."

"Why did you burn my house?" I asked.

"Huh?" he said. "I didn't. The alarms scared me off. Last night I was at home. I didn't do it, Mr. Mason." He began to cry softly.

I looked toward Scott. He hadn't moved from the tree. The moonlight had shifted. His face was now in shadow, but I could see his hands quietly resting in his lap.

"Let's take you home," I said to Bluefield.

Scott slowly rose to his feet and joined us. I couldn't read his face in the flickering light. I listened to the now murmuring sniffles of the teenager. I heard the movement of Scott's body. Felt the occasional breath of wind.

Dan accepted our offer of a ride.

We worked it out. The Porsche didn't have a backseat. Scott would go back to the road, take the Porsche to my place, and come back with my truck. Bluefield gave him directions to the secret entrance.

While we waited, Bluefield hung his head in silence and barely made any movement. I untied him, but he didn't try to run away. I gave him my hanky so he could clean himself up. A half-hour later, I heard the rumble of an engine. Moments later Scott stepped into the light.

We drove with Bluefield between us. The boy didn't say a word. I looked at Scott in the light from the dashboard. His blank expression worried me.

In the truck I asked Dan about his relationship with Jones.

Dan said, "He was a joke. They all were. You were the only one who didn't buy my change. I've done more illegal stuff in the past couple months than in the past four years combined. Jones played like he was my big buddy. Always wanted to do me a favor. Always wanted to talk over everything. He'd talk and be reasonable, and all I had to do was look sincere. Then I'd laugh behind his back, but he was easy to get along with. He never punished me, so I let him be."

"Did you kill him?" I asked.

"No," Dan said.

"Did you see anybody that day after school? Did you go in to talk to him?"

He said he hadn't. He'd come back to talk to Donna Dalrymple.

From the gas station at the corner of LaGrange Road and 191st Street, I called the River's Edge police station. Neither Daniels nor Johnson was on duty. I convinced the guy at the other end of the phone to call one of them at home and have them call the pay phone back. A few minutes later Daniels returned the call. I explained what Dan had told us and where they could find the drugs in the Bluefield house. I told them we'd meet them there.

We arrived before any of the police.

Dan simply opened the door and walked in. Mr. and Mrs. Bluefield sat on a couch in the living room watching television.

All the furniture was new and in prime condition; the television set measured fifty-four inches, the rug was deep and almost sensuous. They jumped at our entrance. Mrs. Bluefield rushed over to Dan. She was a thin woman with hair in a frizz that looked like it had been done by the Wicked Witch of the West. She wore a fringed and beaded deerskin shirt and pants with Day-Glo red moccasins. Dan stood stoically while his mom fussed at him. His dad rushed at us.

He shouted, threatened, and told us to leave.

I said to him, "Aren't you concerned about Dan?"

He glanced at his son. "Kid's a mess. What else is new? I want you and your fruitcake buddy . . ."

He looked at Scott closely for the first time. The silence drew the attention of Dan and Mrs. Bluefield. Mr. Bluefield walked up to Scott. "You're Scott Carpenter, the baseball player."

Scott asked, "Did you burn down our house?"

Mr. Bluefield laughed and sneered. I wasn't ready to beat up another homophobic creep. Scott just looked tired.

I asked, "Did you kill Robert Jones?"

Mr. Bluefield swung toward me and raised his fists. He shouted, "Faggots got no right to ask questions."

The doorbell rang. We all looked at each other. Mr. Bluefield finally moved to answer it. We heard Johnson's voice. Bluefield slammed the door and didn't let him in.

He rushed into the living room. "Cops," he said to his wife. Forgetting us and their son, the two instantly sprang into action. They weren't quite quick enough. Scott dashed to the doorway that led to the rest of the house. Bluefield and wife advanced on him.

Scott crossed his arms in the doorway, his blue eyes radiating cruel ice. The Bluefields hesitated. I heard the cops pounding on the door. I came up behind the Bluefields. "It's over," I said.

Bluefield launched himself at Scott. He never got halfway there. I tackled him, none too gently. We used his own belt to secure him to one of the living-room chairs.

Half an hour later the cops hustled the Bluefields away. Mr. Bluefield had accused us of numerous crimes, but the discovery of the hidden stash silenced him. Turned out the entire ceiling in the bathroom was fake, held down by spring locks controlled by innocuous little buttons in the kitchen.

Johnson and Daniels talked to us in the living room. Daniels said, "They made a lot of accusations. You're real lucky we've been trying to bust them for a long time."

Johnson said, "The kid was awful quiet and subdued. Looked kind of a mess too. You guys do something to him?"

We gave minimal answers and little information. They didn't press the issue. The police had the biggest drug haul in River's Edge history to deal with. Plus they weren't that fond of the kid in the first place. We parted tight-lipped, with the cops warning that they were watching us.

Scott drove the truck back to the city. We didn't speak

until we were in the garage under his building. He shut off the engine and dropped the keys into my hand, but he didn't move to get out. He slumped in the seat, spread his legs wide, crossed his arms over his chest, rested his head against the back cushion, and closed his eyes. He spoke without opening them.

"I just . . . I guess I lost it. I just hated him so much, and I wanted to hurt him. Listening to him describe how he put that stuff on your desk and not caring how it affected you." He opened his eyes and stared out the window at the lines of parked cars.

"Dan Bluefield can bring out that kind of reaction in people," I said.

His hands reached out to grip the steering wheel. "The rush was incredible. I could have ripped his hair out from the roots. I don't know what kept me from banging his head to a pulp. I enjoyed it. I was glad I hit him. Now I feel awful, like you the other day."

I put my hand on his arm. He looked at me. "I guess I really know how you felt the other night," he said.

"We're going to be okay," I said.

"I thought revenge was supposed to feel better than this," he said.

We didn't say much to each other that night. We worked out for over an hour on the machines, Scott still being careful of his pitching arm, me of my wound from Bluefield's knife. He showered first. After I finished, I found him in the electronics room with all the lights off, watching *Casablanca*. The movie was at the scene where they arrest Peter Lorre, and Humphrey Bogart does nothing to help him.

Scott made room for me on the couch. He murmured, "I wanted to lose myself in somebody else's problems for a little while."

We settled into our movie-watching position: pillows propped behind us, legs sprawled on the coffee table, leaning against each other. Usually we have a bowl of popcorn between us, but neither of us was in the mood. I let my mind wander among the characters in the Moroccan desert. For a few minutes I forgot my own troubles. Finally my lack of sleep caught up with me. I woke up with Scott gently nudging me awake. I stumbled into bed and slept ten hours.

That morning we divided up some of his clothes so I would have enough to wear. He hadn't dropped off any of his laundry for the week so I decided to do a couple of loads. I had had an old washer and dryer at my place, which Scott kept in excellent condition and which I used frequently. His utility room contained two gleaming units fit do the work of a family of ten. He rarely used them. Early in our relationship he did a load of our wash together. My underwear came out pink. This I could forgive, but the next week he shrank three of my favorite sweatshirts to unwearability.

I read the paper, drank coffee, and monitored the tumbling clothes. He thumbed through art catalogues, occasionally showing me paintings and asking my opinion. This was one of his methods of finding out what he could get me for Christmas. I didn't let on that I suspected this and made sure I expressed extreme liking for my favorite ones.

A little after noon Sunday we drove out to River's Edge. We had an appointment with Daniels and Johnson at one.

Daniels greeted us with "What the hell did you guys do to the Bluefield kid?"

"He pressing charges?" I asked.

"For what?" Daniels asked.

"What did the kid say?" Scott asked.

Daniels said, "The kid retracted what he said about seeing you, Mason, in the corridor the night of the murder. Said he lied. We were not nice to him about that, by the way. But he looked a little the worse for wear. That social worker showed up. Dalrymple? We left him in her hands."

"Mom and Dad still in jail?" Scott asked.

"Got bailed out early this morning."

"What!" I said.

"Drug money can cover a multitude of sins," Daniels said. "Obviously these two have some connections. The captain told me some fancy lawyer got here an hour after we arrested them. They made bail early this morning. We had to let them go."

A few minutes later we were back on the topic of the murder. "You're still on the front burner on the stove of suspects, but it's not quite as hot as it was. Still . . ." Daniels shook his head.

"What can you tell us about the investigation?" I asked, not expecting much of an answer. But he told us more than I thought he would.

"We're pretty sure the knife came from the school cafeteria," Daniels said. "We checked the brand and it matches the kind they have. Most of the other knives we examined were fairly blunt. This one had been honed. Somebody planned to kill Jones." He told us that nothing in Jones's office had been disturbed, that Jones hadn't been robbed, that according to a careful examination by Carolyn Blackburn and Georgette Constantine nothing was missing or out of place. Neighbors and friends said the Joneses were a good couple, fought perhaps a little less than most. No evidence of extramarital affairs, no abuse, no alcohol, no money problems.

Daniels concluded, "Usually in these cases you count the wife as a major suspect, but this seems almost definitely connected with school."

We nodded agreement.

Daniels said, "We haven't been able to dig up many problems at school. I thought most administrators were assholes. From the way the faculty talked, the guy was a saint."

"He was a good administrator," I said. "We just had disagreements once in a while."

Daniels said, "We checked with your buddy Kurt Campbell to see if there'd been any particular union problems. Nothing out of the ordinary. We did talk to Al Welman, since you and he met with Jones on that grievance, but the old man claims he doesn't know anything."

I hesitated to tell Daniels all we knew. I was still ticked off about the way he and his partner had been treating us. We finished up at the police station, and in the truck Scott said, "Now what?"

I said, "You know what's odd?" I didn't wait for him to answer. "None of our suspects has an alibi for the time the murder could have been committed, but they all have great alibis for burning down the house."

"So none of them did it," Scott said.

"Or somebody's doing a good coverup. . . . I'm pretty convinced Bluefield didn't do it," I said.

"Bluefield dad or kid?" Scott asked. "And are we talking about murder or arson?"

"Arson. The ki— Wait. If the kid didn't burn it, why not the dad?" I explained my reasoning to Scott. "The guy hated me. The kid had to get his homophobia from somewhere, obviously at home, where the idea could be cemented into his head. We didn't ask the father where he was the night of the fire."

"We are not going over to the house to beat him up and get him to confess. Not after yesterday," Scott said.

I didn't contradict that statement. Mr. Bluefield would have to come up with an alibi for Friday night at a later time.

"What about Mr. Bluefield as a murder suspect?" I asked.

"No motive," Scott said. "But if Bluefield or one of the murder suspects burned the house, we're still in danger. Bluefield's got to be pretty pissed at us for busting up his drug concession."

I nodded agreement. Bluefield could be a big problem.

We drove toward my place to get Scott's car. Halfway there Scott said, "I hope this weather holds." It was another gorgeous day.

I said, "I hope we aren't too late to get the color up at the cabin."

He murmured agreement.

"Motive," I said as we pulled into my driveway. I had a hard time looking at the charred remains. "We've got to find out why somebody would kill him. Let's go to the school," I said.

"We are not breaking in," Scott said.

"Who said anything about breaking in? They let one of the local churches use it for Sunday school classes. We shall simply walk in."

"And clues will leap out at us?"

"I want to look around Jones's office, if I can. Maybe I'll be able to spot something of significance the police missed."

Scott gave an audible sigh of resignation. I chose to ignore it.

We pulled up at the school as the congregation began to filter out the doors. We found Georgette, Carolyn Blackburn, and one of the assistant principals, Edwina Jenkins, in the principal's office. They looked startled to see us.

"What are you doing here?" Georgette asked.

We told them about the latest developments with the Bluefields.

Carolyn said, "Edwina is taking over as acting principal tomorrow. We needed to organize a few things."

Edwina wore thick black horn-rimmed glasses. She'd been a physics teacher for ten years and then went back to get her administrative certification. She'd been one of the assistant principals for the past three years.

We chatted for a short while, then walked out of the office. Georgette followed us. She said to Scott, "I didn't want to make a scene in there, but I know you're Scott Carpenter, the baseball player. I go to as many games as I can in the summer. I love watching you pitch. I never thought I'd meet you. I'd heard you and Mr. Mason knew one another. I hardly believed it." She did her most scatterbrained twitter-and-giggle act until she got to the part about wanting specific autographs and specific souvenirs for specific grandchildren.

Carolyn and Edwina left a few minutes later. Carolyn said to Georgette, "Before you leave, be sure to remind Mr. Longfellow that you're gone. That way he won't waste time wondering if you're still here." They left.

"Longfellow works on Sundays?" I asked.

"If you can call it work," Georgette said. "I'll look for him, and he'll be drunk in some corner. I don't tell on him because it's not my business. None of the custodians likes to come in on Sundays, but Longfellow is in trouble because of the other day when you found him asleep. I think they're going to make him go to an alcoholic rehabilitation clinic." She leaned closer to us and whispered, "I hear if that doesn't sober him up they're going to fire him. I don't trust him. I wish they'd fired him years ago."

I said, "Georgette, you could do us a big favor."

"I promised to help you any way I can, and now, with your house burned down . . . anything I can do to help."

"This is pretty serious, Georgette. You don't have to do it if you don't want, and I don't blame you if you get angry at me for asking, but it really might help."

Georgette said, "I could never be angry at you, Mr. Mason."

I know many principals keep an active file on all the teachers in their building. The police might not be aware of it because it was held separate from the official file kept in the district office. I explained to Georgette that I wanted to look in the active teacher files.

She didn't respond for a minute, and I thought I was out of luck. Then she said, "If Mr. Carpenter had some souvenirs in his car, we could run out and get them. You could wait here, Mr. Mason; perhaps even waiting next to that cabinet over there might be more comfortable." She pointed to a file drawer across the room. She paused at the door to the office. "I guess I won't need my purse just walking out to Mr. Carpenter's car." She tossed it on her desk, linked her arm in Scott's, propelled him out the door. She was already twittering at a hummingbird's pace.

For a few seconds I listened to her receding voice and

their departing footsteps. Then I hurried to the cabinet. Locked. Then I realized why Georgette had so elaborately left her purse. I grabbed the keys out of it. Moments later I had the file drawer open. I checked the files of the people we'd talked to. In all of them I found notes that Jones had made about each of their problems. Donna Dalrymple had been caught with Bluefield not once, but twice. I wondered why Jones hadn't simply fired her outright. Al Welman hadn't been completely honest with me, either. Jones had a list of infractions Al had committed for the past six months of school. Next to each problem, Jones had listed the date, the time, and what directive he'd given Welman. Old Al hadn't been a good boy. Jones had listed all his failures to comply with rules: attendance forms not completed, grades turned in late, lesson plans inadequately prepared, and on and on. Al had told me about less than half of them. It's not nice to keep information back from your union rep. Could turn him or her into a fool at meetings with administrators—or, worse, maybe lose you your case because the union rep didn't have all the information. Amazingly enough, in more than half the teacher complaints I've had to handle, the teachers have left out something vital. Something they're ashamed of or embarrassed about. Can't blame them, really. Reputation can be central to a person's life.

On Marshall Longfellow: Jones had caught him in the school basement numerous mornings, sleeping off the effects of alcohol. The guy had gotten drunk at school and never gone home.

I was surprised to find extensive notes on Clarissa Hartwig, the student teacher, and even more to discover that he thought she was totally incompetent and would make an awful teacher. I wondered if he'd told her or the professors at Lincoln University. A report like that could easily endanger her whole career.

Before reaching for the next file I took a quick glance into the hallway. I didn't want Marshall Longfellow accidentally being competent enough to catch me, and I didn't know how long Scott and Georgette would be gone. She was being kind enough to help; I didn't want her to get in trouble if I got caught. I assumed they were doing their best to give me time.

As I riffled through the next file, another concern resurfaced: Maybe the killer was someone from outside the school, to whom we would have no clue, or perhaps one of the other teachers who had problems with him that I didn't know about. I didn't have the time to hunt through all the personnel files. I'd have to stick with Meg's information from the day before, that none of the other school personnel had a motive for murder.

In Max Younger's file, I found that the David Mamet of the Grover Cleveland theater department had directed promising graduates to a shady talent agency in Chicago. Jones had several notes about getting runarounds when he called them. He'd planned to visit them next week.

Fiona Wilson, clotheshorse, woman about town, physics genius, and computer wizard, had offered Jones delights beyond his wildest imaginings while trying to sit on his lap in his office chair.

Jones had been harassing Denise Flowers. The untenured Ms. Flowers had been observed up to four or five times a week, in all of her different classes, and in each one Jones had found flaws. Some of which were preparing lessons poorly, making silly threats of discipline, coming to class late, and glossing over difficult material.

I'd pulled the file drawer all the way out when I first opened it. At the very back was a piece of paper sitting alone and unfiled. I pulled it out. Part of a much larger memo, it started in the middle of a sentence. It was the documentation on Dan Bluefield, including a list of dates and times when Jones had met with the boy or the father or both. After each date was an anecdotal record. I hunted quickly for the rest of the documents.

I heard footsteps coming down the hall. I kept the Bluefield information, stuffed the last folder into its alphabetical place, shut and locked the file drawer, and returned the keys to the purse.

Scott and Georgette walked in smiling a moment later. Georgette took her purse and got ready to leave. I told her that we wanted to interview Marshall Longfellow, so she didn't have to go looking for him.

In the hall after Georgette left, Scott said, "I like her. She's sort of like Meg, only on fast forward. Lot of common sense there. Did you find anything?"

I told him.

"Another round of interviews would seem to be in order," he said.

I agreed.

He examined the Bluefield document briefly. "I don't understand its significance," Scott said.

"I'm not sure there is any," I said, "but I'd like to know where the rest of it is, and I'd like to know what it said. If he was keeping notes on Bluefield, maybe it meant he was going to take action. Maybe he wasn't as big a buddy as Dan thought."

Scott glanced at the notes again. "I don't think this was stuff against the kid," he said. He pointed to the names. "It's about Bluefield senior mostly, not the kid."

"He was after Mr. Bluefield?" I asked.

Scott shrugged. "We could try to check it out, but I can't imagine Bluefield succumbing to our normally irresistible charms."

We found Marshall Longfellow without too much trouble. He was sitting with his back to us in a rusting folding chair on top of the gym roof. I checked there after looking in the heating/air-conditioning room I'd discovered him in on Thursday. He sat far enough away from the edge of the roof so he wouldn't be seen from below, but close enough so he could see all the vista. Walking toward him I saw that from this angle River's Edge looked almost like a peaceful New England town on the ripe edge of fall.

Closer to his chair I noted five or six empty beer cans scattered around him. He'd forgotten his resolve in less

134

than two days. I figured he'd passed out in his drunken state and wasn't moving for that reason. I was wrong. He wasn't moving because he was dead.

Everybody showed up: the cops Daniels and Johnson; the school personnel, led by Carolyn Blackburn and the school-board president; reporters, lurking in the background. The police interviewed us separately and together.

Except for making sure he was dead, we hadn't touched anything. "How'd he die?" I asked. We hadn't been able to see any obvious wounds.

"They don't know yet," Daniels said. "Could be natural causes, but this is another coincidence, and like I said the other day, I don't believe in them. Two deaths in five days in the same school. Your house burned down. Something is definitely screwy."

In their questioning, Daniels and Johnson were polite and correct, but they gave me no reason to trust them or confide in them. Before we left we talked to Carolyn and the school-board president, Jessica Allen.

Carolyn said, "This is sick. The guy wasn't the greatest custodian on earth, but still."

Allen nodded her agreement. She asked, "Are you all right, Mr. Mason? I realize this has been a tough time for you and your friend." She hadn't done a recognition dance after being introduced to Scott.

"As well as can be expected," I said, and thanked her for asking. "Who else was around today?"

"That congregation," Carolyn said. "They'll probably have their own church by next summer. I can't wait. It'll be less of a problem all around. No setting up chairs in the gym, no keeping a custodian on duty."

"I meant, were there any school personnel on duty besides Marshall Longfellow?" I asked.

Carolyn said, "I'd have to check the records, in fact the police asked me to, but as far as I remember, Marshall was it."

"Do you think it was murder?" Jessica Allen asked. She was an attractive, intelligent-looking woman, perhaps in her middle forties.

"I don't know," I said. I didn't want to get into a discussion of murder suspects. A few minutes later we left.

As we sat in the truck Scott said, "This is a revolting development."

I reached over and mussed his hair. "I could use some ideas, not age-old clichés."

"Okay. If it's murder, who profits from Longfellow's death? So far we've got lots of people who benefit from Jones's murder."

"Good question about Longfellow. We don't know anything about his private life," I said. "If he was murdered, it could be for reasons totally unrelated to school."

"Or, he saw something that day and he got killed for what he knew," Scott said.

"Also possible," I said. "For now, the police will check into all that background stuff on him. Maybe Daniels can tell us some later, including how he died. It might not be murder."

We decided to pursue the information contained in the files.

Donna Dalrymple slammed her door in our faces.

Next we tried Al Welman. His excuse for not telling me all the nasty things Jones accused him of was "I forgot."

It is said that the longer people teach, the more they become like the kids in the grade level they deal with, but this was a bit much. He stuck to that excuse. I found myself shouting at him at one point. He had tears in his eyes as he responded, "Don't yell at me. You're one of my few friends. Please stop."

As soon as he said it, I felt rotten for yelling at the poor old guy. We weren't that close. If I was one of his few friends, what must the rest of his life be like?

We told him about Longfellow. He seemed genuinely shocked. Without prompting, Al told us he'd been home alone all afternoon working on the Sunday *New York Times* crossword puzzle.

At the student teacher's house, Ralph Hartwig let us in. He told us he expected Clarissa back any minute from shopping at Orland Square. She'd been gone since eleven in the morning. Plenty of time to get to school to do murder.

We talked baseball for fifteen minutes before the front door opened. Clarissa walked in without any packages. She saw us and threw her keys across the room. She shook a finger at Ralph and yelled, "I told you if they came back, you were not to let them in."

Ralph looked petrified and put upon. He mumbled, "They're only trying to help."

I said, "Marshall Longfellow is dead." That stopped her onslaught for a moment.

"Who is he?" Clarissa asked.

I explained.

"And you came here to find out if I killed him?" she accused.

"No," I said. "We came here to find out if Jones had turned in any reports on you to the university."

Abruptly she plopped onto an ottoman. "He told me he was going to tell my professor at Lincoln University. Jones came in to observe my classes before I was ready. He'd sit there writing for the entire class period. I got so nervous. I forgot kids' names, what I was doing, what questions to ask, what homework to assign. It was chaos."

"When was he going to tell?" I asked.

"I didn't kill him," she said.

"He hadn't done it yet," Scott said.

She gazed at him for a moment, then lowered her head and shook it. She spoke toward the carpet. "He told me he was going to do it this week. Are you going to tell the police?"

"No," Scott said.

We found out she'd had an interview with Jones only a

few minutes before I'd come upon her with Bluefield in the science room.

Ralph said, "I appreciate your not telling the police. Clarissa's had it rough. She's wanted to be a teacher for a long time. He just wasn't fair to her. He never gave her a chance."

We left.

Max Younger wasn't home.

Fiona Wilson met us at the door in a filmy negligee. Strange wear, I thought, for a Sunday afternoon, but then there were days when Scott and I walked around the house all day in our Jockey shorts. Those are often my favorite days.

After she invited us in, Fiona asked if we wanted to accompany her to her bedroom while she slipped into something more appropriate for visiting. She cast many covetous glances at Scott. He didn't seem to notice. He walked over to the top of the television set, picked up a photo in a frame, and asked her, "Who are these people?"

"No one you know," she said, and disappeared down the hallway.

I joined Scott. The picture was of Fiona with what could easily have been a husband or boyfriend; a golden retriever sat in front of them. The picture had been taken in this room.

Fiona's house was typical of the vast majority of the newer sections of River's Edge. One of four types of tract homes offered by a builder with the family room downstairs, kitchen, dining room, and living room on the ground floor, and bedrooms upstairs.

Fiona came back down in a bright pink sweat suit.

Scott and I sat on the couch in the living room. Fiona sat in a purple plush armchair. She swung her legs over the side, put her arms behind her, and threw her head back. I wondered if she desired the effect, which was to emphasize the considerable heft of her breasts. She'd picked the wrong crowd to play for.

I said, "Fiona, what did Robert Jones do when you came on to him in his office?"

She looked startled for only an instant, then slowly ran her bright red fingernails up her thigh and over her abdomen, stopping just short of her ample chest endowment.

She said, "Like all men, he was interested. I enjoy sex and when he came on to me, I figured why not? I can't imagine how you found out, but its your word against mine. He'd be in as much trouble, more even, for coming on to me. So you can take your shady suspicions and shove them up your ass." She delivered this last line with casual defiance.

"Was he blackmailing you?" I asked.

The thought had struck me that with all this negative information about people, Jones might have delved into the monetary possibilities. I didn't think it was much of a theory, but I wanted to check it out.

Fiona uncoiled herself sufficiently so that her feet touched the floor. "Blackmail?" she mused. "No. He knew a few things about me, but everybody knows I like sex. It's not a secret."

"I didn't know," I said.

"It's not for lack of trying."

I looked confused.

She said, "I've come on to you numerous times. You were too naive or too . . ." She stopped a moment, then pointed at Scott. "You guys are lovers. You're gay. No wonder you never noticed." She sat back with her arms crossed over her chest. "That explains a lot."

We asked where she'd been that day. She told us she'd been home alone. A few minutes later, we left, little the wiser for our visit.

Denise Flowers lived in a condo development in River's Edge just south of 167th Street. The area was starkly devoid of trees, and the smoothed-out dirt where lawns belonged testified to the newness of the development.

Denise Flowers greeted us with "Can't you leave me alone?"

I told her about Marshall Longfellow.

She said, "The guy who looks like Santa Claus. He's dead?"

I nodded.

"Why would somebody kill him?" she asked.

"We aren't sure it was murder," I said. "I did find out that Jones was constantly observing you in your classroom and that you weren't going to get tenure this year."

"I want to be left alone," she said. "I don't want to talk about it. I could have been out of a job."

I said, "I'm not trying to bring you trouble, Denise. I'm trying to find out who killed Jones. I'm sorry you were having trouble with him. If you could answer some questions, it might really help."

Ten minutes later, after a lot of cajoling and convincing, she agreed to talk.

She said, "He'd told me that there were problems, but he claimed I had time to correct what I was doing wrong in the classroom. The only thing I ever really did wrong was make him mad at me."

I asked her to explain.

The year before, besides her regular classes and cheerleading duties, he'd asked her to take on extra duties, to help put out the school newspaper and yearbook. At first she had refused. "He told me that I didn't have a choice. That it was a condition of my employment and that I had to do it."

This was probably true. It's often difficult to get teachers to do extra work, so many school districts make it part of the deal in hiring you. The interviewer asks a prospective teacher if he or she is willing to do extra duties. The job seeker, willing to agree to almost anything to get the position, readily acquiesces. Later, this comes back to haunt the new teacher, who is forced to do enormous quantities of work for meager pay.

Denise said, "I'm afraid I got a little snotty with him. I apologized later, but I think even then it was too late. He'd decided to get rid of me no matter what I did."

140

"Was he trying to blackmail you?" I asked.

She looked startled. "No. I haven't got enough money to make it worthwhile for him to ask me for any."

"How did you afford this condo?" I asked. In the south suburbs the price of condos was out of control. She was be in a place that had to be worth well over a $175,000.

"I borrowed from my parents," she said.

"You'd need a job to keep up the payments. A fairly good one," I said.

"That's not your business," she snapped.

"It is if you were desperate enough to kill him to keep your job."

"He'd have passed his notes on to someone," she said. "I'd have tried to destroy the notes, wouldn't I? His documentation on me was devastating."

"Maybe not, if his main reason for getting you fired was that he didn't like you," I said.

She shook her head. "He had enough stuff written down. I couldn't have done a thing about it."

In the car Scott said, "I think she's off the list."

I still wasn't convinced, although she wasn't near the top of my crowd of likely killers.

I picked the Bluefield document out of the glove compartment, where I'd stuffed it after the confusion of Marshall Longfellow's death. "This has got to mean something," I said. "Let's go talk to Bluefield."

8

Scott glared at me. Starting the truck, he turned the key almost hard enough to snap it in two. The tires screeched as we pulled away from Denise Flowers's condo. He didn't speak until five miles later, when we were on Interstate 57.

"That is one of the dumber things you've ever suggested," he said.

Several miles of expressway passed by before the ultimate in witty repartee occurred to me. I said, "Is not."

"Dan Bluefield is not your best friend, the father is a sworn enemy, and the mother isn't going to invite you over for tea any time soon. Why the hell would you want to go over there?"

"I think the Bluefield family is the key to this murder," I said.

"I don't. I think it is foolish and perhaps dangerous for you to go anywhere near anybody in that family."

At the moment I wasn't going near them: Scott was headed home. Other than jumping out of the car while it sped toward Chicago at over sixty miles an hour, I didn't have a lot of options.

We worked out in silence at his place. My arm felt good enough for me to spend an extra half-hour working out my frustration on the rowing machine. Later I found Scott upstairs reading the Sunday paper. We get two sets of the *Chicago Tribune* and *Chicago Sun-Times*. We each read a

142

separate one. I hate it when somebody else reads the paper before I do. We tried various compromises early in our relationship: At first Scott offered to wait until I was finished reading the papers, but eventually I'd find half the sections strewn across the living-room floor on a Sunday morning. Finally he got us separate subscriptions as a first anniversary present.

That night we managed to be civil to each other long enough to order a pizza and eat it. After supper Scott retired to his den to go over the itinerary for a West Coast speaking tour he had scheduled for early November. I sulked in the library, reading *The Eye of the World* by Robert Jordan. I have a weakness for science-fantasy books when upset, and Jordan's opus was one of the best I'd run across in a long while.

At nine the phone rang. I didn't hear Scott stirring, so I answered. Daniels said, "It was murder."

That conclusion was tentative, but Daniels said Longfellow had probably drunk himself into a stupor. Anyone could have come upon him. The man was heavyset and probably a deep sleeper. It would be fairly simple and quick for someone to smother him.

Scott appeared at the library door and looked questioningly at me.

I said to Daniels, "Any idea how long he was dead before we found him?"

"We don't know what time he started drinking. It's going to be hard to tell from the contents of the stomach, I think. My guess is he could have been dead almost any time after he got there. We've got the preacher from the congregation who talked to him about nine. He says Longfellow didn't seem intoxicated. Nobody saw Longfellow after that."

"Not much help," I said.

We talked a few minutes longer.

When I hung up, Scott came and sat next to me on the brown leather couch. He fingered the globe on the table next to the couch. He said, "It's been an emotional week."

"Yeah," I said.

"You know how I get when the season ends."

He hadn't had time to go through his end-of-season depression. We've talked about why he goes through it: missing his buddies who scatter around the country; desire for the excitement of being in front of the crowds; enjoyment of a solid baseball career. Postseason workouts and being on the talk circuit don't make up for the rush of throwing a fastball over ninety miles an hour.

"You haven't had much time to adjust," I said.

He looked at me. "No." He shrugged. "I'm worried about you. I probably shouldn't have come across so strong this afternoon."

"Suggesting going to the Bluefields' was one of my dumber ideas," I said. "I'm sorry I haven't been more attentive to you."

He does need a lot of attention the week or so after the season. His relaxation time culminates when we go up to the cabin in Wisconsin. We hardly say two words to each other the whole time, just spend the three days tramping miles and miles in the woods and along Lake Superior. After the season he's pretty tired and vulnerable, a little like an alcoholic coming down from a six-month drunk, and this year he hadn't had time to crash, because of my problems.

I said, "Next weekend we'll be up at the cabin. I'll make it up to you."

He reached over, pulled me close, and kissed me. I enjoyed his warmth and his after-shower smell. I dropped my hand to the button on his jeans and undid it.

Several hours later we ate cold pizza in the breakfast nook overlooking Lake Michigan and Lake Shore Drive. I take pride in the fact that I'm the one who taught him to enjoy cold pizza, although he still balks at chowing down on it for breakfast. Sometimes it takes so long to train a husband.

I told him what Daniels had said.

144

"Two murders," Scott said. "Longfellow had to die because of something he knew about the first one."

"We need to find out about his personal life," I said. "Maybe he was secretly a spy for the government and foreign agents finally tracked him down."

Scott raised an eyebrow at me. "He was some foreign country's secret weapon to destroy the fabric of society with incompetence? I know: He was part of the first wave of alien invaders destroying society by never fixing anything."

"I am only a little amused," I said.

"And Queen Victoria would be proud," he said.

I chased him around the house, almost caught him in one of the guest bedrooms, and managed to trip him in the living room an inch short of the floor-to-ceiling windows. By this time we were giggling almost uncontrollably, and then we stopped laughing as he pulled me close in a fierce embrace.

The next morning as I swung open my classroom door, a flashing fist whizzed toward my head. I reacted quickly enough to deflect the main impact, but my shoulder took a nasty punch. I rocked back, assumed another punch was coming, and ducked, then dove forward. My head bashed into a lean midsection. At first I guessed it was Dan Bluefield's. I heard the breath whoosh out of my opponent as my charge bashed him against the wall. I backed up. Bluefield Senior, clutching a spot six inches above his crotch, slowly sank to the floor.

I found I still had my briefcase in my left hand. I dropped it on a nearby desk, then turned to examine Bluefield. Other than some ragged gasps for air, he looked hardly the worse for wear.

When he got his breath back, he tried kicking out at me and scrambling to his feet at the same time. A monumentally stupid person would have known he'd try something. Not being monumentally stupid, I sidestepped, twisted around, feinted to my left, caught my balance, and brought my foot up into his crotch. Another round to Mason.

"What can I do for you, Mr. Bluefield?" I asked.

He grasped his nuts and moaned.

"Did you come to confess to killing Jones and Longfellow? Longfellow saw you sneaking around the night of the murder. He could have turned you in. Of course, how would you know he knew?" I said this last part more to myself.

"Who's Longfellow?" Bluefield asked.

"Old custodian around here." His lack of knowledge seemed genuine.

"Think you're a smart guy, don't you?" he gasped.

"I'm not the one in this room with the bruised balls," I said.

"You ruined me," he said.

"The pain will go away. I'm sure you'll be able to orgasm again soon. Maybe father a few more darlings like Danboy."

"The drugs, you stupid shit. My supplier cut me off. He won't pay any of my legal fees."

"I'm heartbroken."

Bluefield eased himself into a chair. I kept my distance so I'd have plenty of time to ward off any surprise attacks.

"You're going to be sorry you ever messed with me or my kid."

"I've heard that tune. But if your supplier abandoned you, who posted your bail?"

"I've got a few other connections."

"Why is Dan such a mess?" I asked.

"He's not a mess."

"I checked the records. Arrested for the first time at eleven. In three different chemical rehab programs before the age of fifteen. Almost nineteen years old and he barely qualified to be a senior this year, and I suspect that came about because Donna Dalrymple pulled a few strings."

Bluefield snorted, "My kid told me he was pulling her string. I'm proud of him. I made it with a couple of my teachers when I was in high school." I noted his build and physique, tried to imagine him as a teenager. I guessed he was in his mid- to late thirties; he would have been in his late teens when he fathered Dan, would have had Dan's stringy muscularity. The face probably wouldn't have had as many nicks and scars then—results, I assumed, of choosing to fight instead of negotiate his way out of difficulties.

"Did you know Mr. Jones was keeping a file on you and your kid?"

He looked confused. "Why should I care about some file some wimp principal kept? Makes no difference to me. He's dead anyway."

"Why are you here?" I asked.

"I came to beat the shit out of a fucking faggot."

"That makes no sense," I said. "With all the school personnel around, you couldn't hope to get away with it."

He gave me a blank look. I could see Dan had inherited his dad's brains, and the old man didn't have that many to spare in the first place.

"Mr. Bluefield, why don't you get the fuck out of my life? If you let your kid alone, he might have a chance at a decent life."

"That was Scott Carpenter with you on Saturday," he said.

I decided to flow with his change of topic by giving him a yes.

"He's a faggot like you."

I said, "You don't get to say faggot any more in my presence. I'll beat the shit out of you next time, and any other time you say it."

He stood up. "I'm going to call all the newspapers and tell them Scott Carpenter diddles with guys."

I said, "They already know."

He looked confused.

"Do you really think people you've worked with for a while don't guess when someone's gay? Do you think reporters who've covered the team for years haven't figured

it out? This closet shit is getting pretty old. You're way
behind the times."

"You're lying," Bluefield snarled.

I sighed. "Kids are going to be coming in here in a few
minutes. You have anything sane to say to me or are you
going to blow stupidity out of your ass until I die of bore-
dom?"

He looked resentful and rebellious at this, but for the
moment he refrained from an outright attack.

"When did you get out on bail?" I asked.

"Why?"

"Just want to know if you got out in time to have killed
Marshall Longfellow."

"I never got near the old guy. I got out of jail and spent
the day in the city trying all my contacts. I lost a lot of my
stock because of you and I need to be staked again. You
cost me a bundle of money. I may have to move out of
town. I came to beat the money out of you, or your pretty
buddy."

"Get real. I have no fear of you or anything you could
possibly do."

I guess he objected to my arrogance, because he bellowed with rage and launched himself at me. I stepped
aside and he flew past me, tripped, and landed against a
corner of my desk. His face rammed into the edge of it at
almost full tilt. He staggered to the floor, clutching the
desk, attempting to keep himself upright. I saw a few drops
of blood seep from a cut just over his eye.

I watched him put his other hand out toward the chalkboard, steady himself, then lurch or stumble toward the
doorway. "I'll be back to make you pay, faggot," was his
parting shot.

I took a step in his direction. He nearly tripped on his
own feet as he retreated out the door.

After a surprisingly ordinary run of morning classes, I
hunted up Meg at lunch and told her about Bluefield's visit.
Her comments about the elder male idiot in the Bluefield
clan were not positive. I sketched out for her a plan I had

for dealing with Donna Dalrymple: Meg would go with me to confront the school psychiatrist and act as a buffer. She readily agreed.

On the way to Donna's office Meg asked me how I was handling the pressure of teaching, losing my house, being involved in a murder, and dealing with the Bluefields. I told her the kids in class were okay and that Scott generally managed to keep me on an even keel.

We found Donna Dalrymple at her desk in her office, munching on cookies and sipping a Diet Coke. A Mrs. Fields bag open on the desk attested to her excellent choice in cookie companies. Somebody who eats white-chocolate-chip cookies for lunch can't be all bad.

She eyed Meg warily as we entered the room, then spotted me and jumped to her feet.

"I won't stay in the same room with that man," she said. "I'll call the superintendent. Get out."

Meg said, "Donna, you're out of control. You used to be able to handle yourself. Do you really want to be a sniveling woman who loses her sense of self just because she's under an emotional strain? I've seen how you've worked all these years. I know you're not that kind. We've talked. We used to be good friends."

"I can't talk with him here."

"Want me to leave?" I asked. Meg nodded.

I went to call Scott to see if he'd had any luck with the Paradise Agency for Young Actors and Actresses, the talent agency whose name I'd found in Jones's files.

He told me he'd visited them just after they opened up at nine. They had an office on south Michigan Avenue just a half-block north of the old Lexington Hotel, where Geraldo Rivera hadn't found anything in Al Capone's vault.

"You wouldn't believe the building," Scott said. "It was a two-story brick affair built maybe around 1910. I walked in and saw rats glare at me as if I were the one who needed to be exterminated. They didn't seem to be worried about my harming them. These were industrial-strength critters."

149

"Did you get to the agency?" I asked. Sometimes his stories unravel slowly enough to drive me nuts.

He took me up the befouled stairs, through a door with cracked glass, to a cubicle too filthy even for the rats to live in. In the middle of a mound of dirt and grime that might once have been a desk with papers on it, sat a handsome man in an impeccable suit.

"The guy was gorgeous," my lover said. "The suit was cut perfectly."

"How nice for him and the suit," I said.

Scott ignored my sarcasm. "His name was Blane Farnsworth. He recognized me right away. He told me not to be put off by the office. They'd lost their lease on the last place, and the new one wasn't ready. He tried to sign me up as a client. I declined."

Scott'd asked the guy about Max Younger. Farnsworth claimed he never heard of a Max Younger. Checked some files and said the name wasn't listed. "I think he was lying," Scott finished.

"Any way you can check him and his agency out?"

"Way ahead of you. I called my agent."

Scott's agent, Beauregard Vincent Strong, was head-quartered in Los Angeles. I'd never met him. Scott generally described him as an acceptable weasel.

"I woke him up at home. He promised to check and get back to me later this afternoon."

I told him about the Bluefield visit and promised to meet him in the city as soon as I was done talking to people at school.

I didn't have time to find out what Meg had learned from her talk with Dalrymple, because the bell rang for afternoon classes. I spent two impatient periods waiting. When the bell rang for my planning hour, I hurried to the library and asked what had happened. Meg said we needed to talk to Donna together.

Just before we entered the room, Meg said, "Donna and I used to be good friends, but we drifted apart. We talked this noon about many things."

We found Donna expecting us in her office. She looked puffy-eyed.

I leaned my shoulder against the door. Meg propped herself against the wall on my right. Dalrymple sat on my left.

While Meg talked Donna stared at her hands, which were clutched together in front of her on the desktop. Meg spoke briefly about the need for solving the murder, about not wanting to threaten Donna, and about how I was a person who could be trusted. When she finished, Donna gave a tremendous sigh and looked up at me.

She explained how her relationship with Dan grew over time. The heart of her remembrance came when she said, "Dan has a lot of hate in him. It's directed toward his father. A lot of Dan's acting out is trying to compensate, to work out his feelings. At any rate, the father is the root cause of a lot of Dan's problems. We finally had a significant breakthrough the first week of school this year." She'd started working with Dan all of last term. They'd talked three or four times a week. He'd started out hostile and uncommunicative. "That started to change after he had to spend two months at a work-release program instead of going to jail for two months this summer for stealing some kid's motorcycle. It was a big misunderstanding. The kid told him he could borrow it, but Dan has an awful reputation around the courthouse and he got a nasty judge."

While he was on a work detail on a remote country road, the three crew members with him had almost succeeded in raping him. He'd managed to run away dressed in only his socks and T-shirt. "The experience hit him hard. I was a little surprised when he opened up about it."

"He's not gay?" Meg asked.

"No, but I think the attempted rape contributed a lot to his hatred for you, Mr. Mason. I didn't make the connection until I talked to Meg today. I suppose I should have earlier, especially after our talk last week." Donna shrugged. "I was more concerned about him opening up to me, and he did. He certainly couldn't open up to anyone at home about the incident, and I doubt he could trust any of his friends. He could lose status if that kind of thing got out. He cried for nearly half an hour, and what he kept saying was 'I hate him.' At first I thought he meant one of his attackers, but it was his dad."

Over the next few weeks, as Dalrymple and Bluefield talked, they became closer. "I don't know how it happened. I know it was my fault because I'm the adult."

"The kid was eighteen," Meg said.

"That's why Jones didn't fire me outright," Donna said. "But it was unprofessional of me. I shouldn't have, and I shouldn't have done anything at school. It was stupid."

The details of how the affair got started weren't terribly important, so I didn't ask.

"I didn't kill Jones," she said. "I met with him that day and agreed to a plan for me to leave honorably. I told Dan that day that I wouldn't be able to see him anymore. Dan was furious. I'm sure that's why he attacked the student teacher and you. I was stupid to cut off the relationship, but I didn't see any other way out. When he came back from the doctor after your fight, he came to see me. I felt such guilt. I held him and comforted him."

"You didn't . . . ?" Meg asked.

"No." Dalrymple sounded totally miserable. "My husband doesn't know about any of this. I want to protect him and the children. I'm leaving the state. I'm going to practice somewhere else. It'll probably mean I have to tell my husband the truth. He'll demand a divorce. Not that that would be a shock. Dan was more satisfying in this room than my husband was in the ten years we were married."

She opened her desk drawer and pulled out a manila folder. "I wrote to this place the first time I got caught with Dan. I got the answer the day before the murder."

She showed us an acceptance of her application at a clinic in Denver. "They took me quickly because the professor I did my residency with at Northern Illinois University is the head of the program. He's often asked me to come out to join his staff. I had no reason to kill Jones. I was out of it."

We left her minutes later. In the hallway Meg said, "Poor thing. I feel sorry for her."

After school I found Max Younger ordering kids about the auditorium. I jumped onto the stage to talk to him. He told me he had a show to do, and he could give me five minutes between rehearsals of acts two and three about four o'clock. I grabbed his arm and whispered in his ear, "Paradise Agency for Young Actors and Actresses."

He turned red, barked a few orders to the assembled kids, and beckoned me off the stage. We sat in the last row of the auditorium.

"What's the meaning of this?" he demanded.

"I know the name of the agency, and that you were connected with it. I know Jones was investigating. I know there was something shady about the operation." This last was a bit of a lie. "I want to know what was so shady, exactly, and how Jones found out about it."

He chose to call my bluff. "Jones didn't know shit and neither do you."

I said, "I think there's something to know. Something that you could get in big trouble for. Something big enough for you to want to kill Jones."

He jumped to his feet and leaned toward me, shaking a finger in my face. "I have done nothing wrong, nothing anybody can prove is wrong, so butt out of my life." He stomped back to the stage. Seeing it was useless to pursue the topic, I left.

I returned to the city. Scott met me in the entranceway of his apartment. "I just got a call from my agent. The Paradise Agency has a nasty reputation." Beauregard had told him about rumors that Paradise hired young actors and actresses to perform overseas, mostly in Italy and Japan, but other places as well. "Some people talk about kids never coming back."

"I thought white slavery was a thing of the past," I said.

"Beauregard couldn't give me any confirmation of the

rumors. He didn't remember where he heard them. Paradise has branches in New York, L.A., and Atlanta. I described the place here to him. Beauregard seemed to think they were all probably like that."

"Let's pay them another visit," I said.

If anything, Scott had understated the filth and degradation of the building and the surroundings. We paused in the alley next door to reconnoiter. I never wanted to explore the alley's depths. This was Urban Nightmare Number One, first-class and done right. Scott was right about the enormous rats.

Blane Farnsworth had a nameplate on his desk. He saw Scott, stood up, and held out his hand. "You changed your mind. You came back to sign up." Scott was right. The suit fit him beautifully. The guy was a hunk.

Scott shook Farnsworth's hand and introduced me. I got a puzzled look and a handshake. I glanced around the room. It was the kind of office that Miss Havisham would have felt at home in.

Scott and I had decided on a strategy on the way over. We'd start nice. Scott said, "I thought about your offer and decided I wanted to know what you could do for me."

Farnsworth gave us a glowing picture of what he could do, then said, "With you as a client we'd be able to move right up."

We sat in unmatched kitchen chairs that had been patched with duct tape. Scott asked about the agency's current list of clients.

Farnsworth reeled off a list of unfamiliar names and bookings in places I'd never heard of.

I told him that.

Farnsworth said, "I don't quite understand your presence here." He sounded puzzled and suave, but I thought I detected irritation and suspicion just below the surface.

Scott said, "He's my lover and we want to know how you would handle our relationship as a coming-out thing in the papers. We're thinking of getting married on Johnny Carson."

"Like Tiny Tim did?" Farnsworth asked.

Tiny Tim was a star briefly in the late sixties. He played ukulele and sang songs in a grating falsetto. He got married to a Miss Vicky on the Carson show, which that night drew one of the highest ratings in its history.

Scott said, "I'm sure it would draw a lot of viewers. Could really put this agency on the map."

I could almost see little dollar signs rolling in Farnsworth's eyes. They'd stop and hit the jackpot in a second. He said, "You're really gay? You guys look so masculine. Are you putting me on?"

Scott leaned over and kissed me on the lips.

The guy said, "Wow. Scott Carpenter in my office, kissing a guy. Wow." He shook his head.

"Can you handle the bookings and publicity?" Scott asked.

"I guess, sure. Definitely." He gained momentum with each utterance. He began to outline plans for press conferences, speaking engagements, national and international tours.

"One thing," Scott said.

"Anything," Farnsworth said.

"We need some information," Scott said.

Farnsworth looked wary. "I told you this morning that I didn't know the guy you asked about."

Scott said, "You don't tell us, you don't get the contract."

Farnsworth's look turned from wary to definitely suspicious. His handsome face bent into frown lines. "This is a put-on to get information. You don't need a dinky little operation like this. You've got big-time agencies behind you. What the hell is this? And don't give me any of this 'I'm sorry for a small agency and want to give it a chance.'"

I couldn't think of any arguments to allay his suspicions. Judging from Scott's silence, neither could he.

Farnsworth rummaged in his desk and pulled out a

gleaming gun. He said, "I want answers from you two, before I throw you out."

I checked the distance to the door, and wondered whether it would be possible to create a diversion or whether a frontal attack was feasible.

Farnsworth caught my eye. "Don't even think about it. No matter what noise you make, help won't come. Nobody in this neighborhood cares, and if they do, they know enough not to ask questions."

"You wouldn't murder Scott Carpenter," I said.

He gave me a nasty grin. "Wouldn't I? I want some answers." He demanded to know what we really wanted. Scott repeated what he'd said this morning.

Farnsworth said, "You keep mentioning this Younger guy. I told you I never heard of him. I want you to leave." He waved the gun at us. We got up and edged toward the exit. "Don't come back," he warned. We slipped out the door.

In the street Scott said, "Cute can cover a multitude of sins, but I'd never trust him."

"Let's wait for him to come out," I said.

"For what? If we follow him, he'll probably just go home like most of the other commuters in the city."

"I'd like to look around his office without the benefit of his assistance," I said.

"Now look—" Scott began.

Quickly I pulled him into the alley. Farnsworth was at the door to his building. His tie was loosened and he carried a paperback book with him.

In the filth-infested alley we debated. Scott didn't want to go in and had several excellent reasons why we shouldn't. "It's illegal. We have no proof he's done anything wrong. We could get caught."

I had no answer to his arguments, so I marched out of the alley and back to the building entrance. I walked up the stairs. Scott was behind me, muttering and cursing. His most frequent comment was "This is the dumbest thing we've ever done together." I heard occasional noises from a few of the other cubicles in the building. On the second floor no light shone from inside the Paradise Agency. Breaking in was simple: I gave the door an angry shove and it burst open. I managed to catch it before it slammed into the wall. We rummaged around the grime and filth for half an hour. It wasn't five yet, and the window faced west across Michigan Avenue, so we didn't have to turn the light on.

Scott whispered, "Let's get the hell out of here," an exasperatingly high number of times.

Just after I said, "Would you shut up?" we heard footsteps coming toward the door.

He growled and I murmured, "Hush."

The footsteps stopped outside the door. I'd closed and tried to relock it. Whoever it was used the same method I did to enter: a sharp shove on the door, and a grab before it banged into the wall behind it. Max Younger stood in the doorway with a McDonald's bag in one hand and an astonished look on his face.

We gazed at each other for a moment. He glanced at Scott. "You're somebody," Max said to him.

I said, "What the hell are you doing here?"

Max trudged into the room, flipped on the desk lamp, dropped his bag of burgers onto the desk, and flopped into the chair.

I said, "I want answers now, Max. What the hell is this operation?"

Max decided on exasperation as a major part of his response. He said, "It's a second job. What the hell does it look like? If I ever want to pay back what I owe the district, I have to get it somewhere. I moonlight here. Farnsworth called me early today and told me you'd been around. I didn't know you'd try to break in. I should call the cops."

"I bet they'd love to look at your files," Scott said.

"They wouldn't find anything," Max said. "We haven't made a dime in six months. We had to move from our last place. We can barely pay the rent on this fleabag office."

"If it doesn't make any money, how will that help you pay what you owe?" I asked.

"We're expecting a couple of things to break for us real soon."

He ignored the skeptical look on my face. "Then what did Jones find?" I asked.

Max sighed. "He found rumors. He'd read some article in some tabloid talking about phony agencies. He believed them. I suppose I didn't help much by telling him it was none of his business. I guess he got suspicious, but there wasn't anything for him to find, because there's nothing here. Sure, we get kids bookings overseas, but they're all legit, and all the kids come back."

"Mind if we check?" I asked.

Max hesitated, then said, "Oh, hell. I don't care. Do what you want. You won't find anything."

I didn't think we would. They probably wouldn't keep records like "Teenager sold into slavery, $100, see Omar the Tentmaker in Ashtrakan."

"Where else do you keep files?" I asked.

"Hidden around the city in locked luggage containers at the train stations and bus depots," Max said. "We move them every twenty-four hours. Good luck finding them all."

I didn't appreciate his sarcasm, but I guess we didn't have much choice. We weren't prepared to search the city. Certainly he wasn't prepared to give us any more information.

"Didn't work," I murmured as I started the truck.

"What we need to do is have one of those murder-mystery scenes," Scott said. "You know, where they gather all the suspects together? We explain how it logically has to be one of them, and then one of the others dramatically stands up and confesses to having been the murderer."

I swung east onto Balbo Drive to get to Lake Shore Drive.

Scott continued, "We could find some way to trick them into confessing."

"Maybe you've hit on the right approach," I said.

"I was making a joke," Scott said. He glared at me. "I can already tell I'm not going to like this."

"Yes, you will." I outlined my plan as we cruised up Lake Shore Drive. It was simplicity itself. We would tell all the suspects that we knew that Jones had had more files hidden somewhere in the office and that we were assembling a detail to take the place apart to find them the next evening after school. I said, "Jones had to have something on the murderer that we haven't uncovered. The murderer will have to come to find and destroy it sometime tomorrow after school."

Scott's objections began with, Won't they get suspicious? How do you know there really is something? Won't they be afraid of being caught? How are we going to get the school to cooperate? And went on beyond. He even threw in "Let's just call the police" a couple of times.

The man has no imagination, or too much. He alternated between realistic roadblocks and fanciful fears.

At home I called Meg. She was more than willing to join in the conspiracy. In fact she offered to help make sure each of the suspects knew about the supposed search.

About being caught setting the trap, I said, "I have a right to be in the school, and I don't feel guilty about trying to trap a murderer. I've been a suspect far too long."

To Scott's objection that there might be nothing to be found I said, "These people all had guilty secrets. Who knows what else Jones might have found out? My bet is they'll all assume the worst, or at least the killer will. They'll panic easily."

Scott again urged calling the police.

"They don't even know about these people," I said.

"Which brings up another point," he said.

We wrangled on the police issue. Finally I said, "Frank's on vacation. Those other two cops haven't been sympathetic. They aren't interested in getting me off the hook. Only we are. We've got to do everything we can. If Daniels and Johnson go talk to those people, they'll just deny anything they said to us. I think we have to give this a try."

Next day at noon, Meg and I compared notes. We knew for certain that all our suspects had heard the news. When Scott showed up at four, the three of us discussed details. He still had lots of objections, but with both Meg and me against him, he soon gave up.

The murderer couldn't try anything until after the office closed at five. We'd taken Georgette into our confidence. She made sure someone was in the office at all times to prevent the murderer from looking around during the day. She also arranged it so that the custodians would be in the new section all afternoon and night, working on tasks far from the office.

I figured the murderer would try earlier than later. We'd announced the new inspection wouldn't happen until tomorrow. Plus, the earlier whoever it was showed up, the less likely his or her appearance would draw attention.

The last rays of golden sunlight peeked through nooks and crannies as we moved into position. Like the people we expected after us, we avoided the night custodians. It wasn't hard. We heard them in the new section with a radio blaring and vacuum cleaners distantly humming. As we moved toward our objective, the noise slowly faded.

We took our position in the washroom directly across the hall from the main office. I climbed onto one of the toilets and carefully removed a ceiling tile. Now we could peer through the uncurtained glass walls of the office. From the hall or the office you could only see a few inches of missing tile. And we were high up, where people didn't normally look.

The light wasn't as bad as I thought it might be. Exit signs gleamed at corridor junctions, illuminating the way to various wings of the campus. Occasionally the gleam from the headlights of cars pulling into the circular drive swept across the blinds in the windows at the far end of the office.

We had a perfect spot, with only one major drawback: To remain in our perch we had straddle dividers between the johns. This became excessively uncomfortable, since we tried to move as little as possible. An hour and a half later each movement of muscle became near agony. We were in good shape, but the tension on one set of muscles for a prolonged period was hell.

It didn't help that fifteen minutes after we started, Scott began to get mutinous. By the time the hour and a half was up I would have cheerfully made him walk the plank and spread shark food on the waters to make sure he'd be the main course for dinner when he hit the water.

He'd begun another "I told you this was a waste of time" crack when I thought I heard something. The custodial noises had long since dimmed to nothingness.

I placed a hand on his shoulder. He'd been grousing in a whisper and fell silent immediately. I waited a minute without hearing a repetition. I was almost ready to whisper to Scott when the noise came again. Definitely the sound of somebody easing down the corridor and trying to remain silent. In the darkness I couldn't see which direction this someone was coming from, and my range of vision was limited.

I listened with remembered jungle instincts, then pointed to the right. A dark mass crept slowly along next to the wall. Its path would take it directly beneath us. We couldn't risk moving.

◣ 9 ◢

Along with a rush of adrenaline, I felt an enormous surge of satisfaction. The killer had walked right into our trap.

I watched the form creep to a spot almost under us. I saw the head turn back and forth, checking both ways in the corridor. Slowly the figure crept across the hallway. I could see long hair sway, and guessed our sneak was Fiona Wilson. At the door to the office she paused. A few moments' fumbling followed. In the light from the exit sign above the office door I saw her working at the lock. My eyes had adjusted enough to the dimness that I could make out her features and see that she wore a designer jogging outfit, appropriately black for hiding in shadows.

I didn't want to jump out at her until she'd had time to get into the office and do some searching. Maybe she'd even find something that would convict her more surely than her presence already did.

I heard a soft click; the office door swung open and she tiptoed inside. I watched her flick on a flashlight. It shone briefly. She inched her way to the file cabinet I had examined earlier, eased it open, and placed her flashlight so it shone only a narrow beam of light toward what she was reading.

I motioned to Scott. He put his ear next to my mouth. I said, "Let's move out."

His soft footfall hit the tile floor. At the same moment I

thought I heard another noise. I glanced quickly toward Fiona. She continued to peruse the files. I inspected the corridor in both directions. A small blob had appeared at the entrance to the north corridor. The mass of greater darkness could have been a head peering around the corner.

"Scott," I whispered. "I think there's another one."

He carefully scrambled back up next to me. By straining he could follow my gaze.

"Ah nuts," was his profound comment.

The new interloper flattened itself against the corridor. From the size, I suspected it was Al Welman. Light gleamed from distant exit signs enough so I could see the reflection on the bald head of the old English teacher as he neared the office.

Welman was ten feet from the office when he slipped and banged his hand against a locker. I looked across at Fiona. She'd heard it. Her flashlight flicked off. I could make out her shape as she disappeared farther into the office. I thought I saw the door to the office of the dean of students open and shut.

I glanced back at Welman. He stood as if paralyzed, one hand dangling an inch from where it had struck the locker. Suddenly he swiveled his head from left to right, then rushed toward the office door. He fumbled with the knob for a second. Fiona must have left it unlocked, because in only a second, Welman was in the office. He crouched down behind the counter. For five minutes he didn't move.

Finally I saw his gleaming dome slowly inch its way above the top of the counter. His eyes searched intently out the office windows for possible danger. A minute later, he retreated to the same file cabinet as Fiona. Out came a flashlight and he began the same sort of inspection.

"Okay, Sherlock," Scott said. "You caught two of them. Not bad. Now what?"

"I'm not sure." I eased my back against the wall in the john. Numerous unhappy muscle groups protested the rigid position I'd kept them in.

Scott tapped my shoulder. He pointed.

I joined him at the observation post and followed the direction of his finger. Down the hallway from the right crept another figure.

"Damn."

"My sentiments exactly," Scott said.

I looked across at Welman. He turned off his flashlight, shut the file drawer, crouched, and moved back toward the counter. I lost sight of him for a few seconds; then he reappeared. He moved toward the inner offices. I wondered what would happen if he ran into Fiona, but he passed up the dean's office, instead opening the door to Jones's. He flicked on his flashlight.

At the same moment our new person reached the office door. The noise he or she made opening it alerted Welman. His light flicked off and he quickly swung Jones's door shut. The angle from the main office door made it difficult for the third intruder to see Jones's office, so he or she didn't notice the brief flicker of light, or maybe thought it was the gleam from a car pulling into the drive in front of the school.

The new person made the same beeline to the file cabinet. There was a hood over the face, but from the movements and general build I guessed it was Max Younger. Another flashlight. At the rate we were going, by morning there wouldn't be another battery left in River's Edge. More searching through the files.

I'd resigned myself to futility by this point.

When the next noise came, from another furtively creeping figure—a large one this time—I almost expected it.

Max had had plenty of time to go through the files, however, and had started on the office storage room. I knew that was where they kept the district records. He propped the door open an inch, probably so he could hear anyone approaching, so he was prepared when the new person lost his or her footing. That's when I realized that the hulking mass seemed to be two people. Possibly they'd tripped over each other's feet. They scrambled up and

164

seemed prepared to flee, when we all heard loud clunking sounds approaching from the new wing.

The two—I could see now that they were Clarissa and Ralph Hartwig—hurried to the office and crouched behind the counter as one of the custodians, whistling cheerfully, dragged a mop and bucket behind him. He made enough noise so that all the hidden suspects must have heard him.

A moment later the Hartwigs were thumbing urgently through the files.

Donna Dalrymple and Denise Flowers showed up five minutes after that. The Hartwigs only had time to hide behind the counter. Donna and Denise nearly tripped over them.

I decided it was time for an appearance.

We climbed down and made our way to the office. We could see the flashlights and hear wrangling voices. I opened the office door and flipped on the light switch. It didn't make a lot of difference if the custodians or someone else found us now. We had all our guilty suspects right where we wanted them—sort of.

I invited all the searchers into Jones's office. They spent the next five minutes in shouts and accusations. I sat behind the desk while Scott leaned on the window ledge behind me. Arrayed in chairs in front of us were the six suspects.

Good, I thought, this is where I reveal the damaging evidence about who really did it. Or they jump up and tell all. But the defiant and angry people in front of me didn't give off the slightest hint of guilt or willingness to confess. Worse, I couldn't think of a thing to say. "Caught you now" seemed inadequate.

When they all paused for a moment, Scott said, "Why did you all come here?"

No one said a word.

Scott said, "You all had reason to kill Jones, and you all obviously had something to hide that we haven't found out yet. Eventually we, or the police, will find that out. Why not get it out in the open now?"

His voice thrummed almost musically. I caught that hint of a Southern drawl I enjoyed so much.

Only Donna Dalrymple spoke. "Mason had a reason to kill him, too. He's just trying to get himself off the hook. This was a cheap stunt that I, for one, am not going to put up with. I'm leaving."

"Leaving could make it look as if you had something to hide. We know you did, because you showed up. Leaving won't help," I said.

She returned to her chair.

To the group at large I said, "Coming here makes you all look guilty. One of us is a murderer. We need to find out everybody's motives, including yours, Donna."

"Well, I didn't do it," Ralph Hartwig said. "I'd never even met the guy."

Al Welman laughed. He said, "You set this up, Mason. You thought you were smart. Figured the guilty one would show up. Instead, all of us are here, and you aren't anywhere near a solution."

"We should talk about what Mason has to hide," Max said.

"What?" several people asked.

He pointed at me. "He's gay and he's got a lover."

"Why would I care if people found out I was gay?" I asked. "Most everybody here knows. I've got nothing to hide. Besides my lover is rich enough to buy all of our salaries for the past twenty years."

"Loss of prestige," Dalrymple said immediately. "Everybody is afraid of that. You aren't immune."

I opened my mouth to let off some frustration and anger, but Scott said, "Hold it, everybody. So we know Tom's possible motive. He denies it, and I, of course, agree with him. What about the rest of you? It's time for all the secrets to be out on the table."

We got lots of nasty cracks and arguments, but no cooperation.

Suddenly the door opened and Carolyn Blackburn marched into the room with Meg right behind her.

Carolyn said, "The custodians called. Said there were lights on in the office that weren't supposed to be on." She sighed. "The general rule they have is to call rather than put themselves in danger. They aren't the brightest. What's going on?"

Meg said, "I saw Carolyn walk in, Tom. I decided it would be better if I followed."

I explained to Carolyn how I had had the rumor spread during the school day, and how we'd planned to catch the murderer by seeing who came looking for further information.

When I finished, Carolyn gave a faint smile. "Didn't work." She glanced around at the assembly. "I think it's time you all told me what it is you're hiding."

Scott brought chairs in from the outer office for Carolyn and Meg. They got settled. None of the suspects seemed willing to start.

"I know a great deal about each of you that I promised not to tell," I said. "It would be more graceful if we heard it from you rather than me."

No response.

Carolyn said, "All your secrets must be pretty awful if you can't tell."

Ralph Hartwig said, "Mason is gay."

Carolyn said, "I figured that out a week after I entered the district. So what?"

"Maybe she's in the conspiracy with Mason." This was Al Welman's contribution.

Carolyn frowned at him. "Conspiracy to do what? I have nothing to gain by Jones's death. I was in a meeting from one that afternoon until after seven with all the state legislators who have constituencies in the school district."

Max Younger said, "I think one thing is clear. Whatever Jones knew, he didn't tell Carolyn Blackburn. We can all breathe easier. If she knew something, she'd tell us now."

Carolyn said, "I don't know anything. Is there something for me to know?"

I said, "Yes."

She looked at each of them in turn, then back at me. "Obviously no one is going to tell. I think it's time to bring the police in on this."

This engendered a round of vigorous protests, which Meg interrupted after five minutes. "Maybe Jones did keep separate records somewhere in the office. Everybody was looking for them. Maybe all we need to do is find them. Obviously there wasn't a set for Carolyn to find or all your secrets would be out."

For over an hour Carolyn and Meg searched through every part of the many offices. The rest of us sat in Jones's office, avoiding one another's eyes.

Finally Carolyn slumped into the chair behind Jones's desk. "Nothing," she said, and drew a deep breath. "It's very simple. You all tell me or I call the police."

No one said anything for a full minute.

"Fine," she said, and reached for the phone.

Clarissa Hartwig placed her hand over the receiver. "I'll tell. I don't want the police, but I don't want to talk in front of all these people."

We arranged to talk to each person separately. Meg waited with them in the main office while Carolyn, Scott, and I interviewed each one in Jones's office.

Clarissa told Carolyn about her awful evaluations and Jones's warning that he would tell her supervisor. "I came back tonight because I was afraid he'd already written the letter. I knew my supervisor hadn't gotten it. After I heard the rumors today, I had to give it a try. I could have lost my whole career."

Carolyn said, "You'll be evaluated again."

Clarissa said, "You mean I'll have a chance?"

"You'll be evaluated fairly, like anyone else," Carolyn said. "If it turns out Jones was right, the report will reflect that."

The young woman slumped in her chair.

Carolyn explained to each of the reluctant others, "It's me or the police. Mason already knows you'd make good murder suspects. He'll be made to tell all he's found out.

I can minimize the scandal here and now, but not if the police are called in. In fact, I promise to do what I can to protect you."

One by one they talked. Max confessed that one of the kids he'd sent to the Paradise Agency this summer had disappeared in Hong Kong and hadn't been heard from in three months. Jones had found out. Fiona had been making anonymous calls to Jones's wife, saying he was cheating on her. Jones had a tap put on his phone and had caught her. Al Welman confessed to trying to increase his pension. He attempted to have the district bookkeeper report his income higher than it was. The bookkeeper had reported this to Jones. Denise Flowers said that since she knew she was going to be fired she'd started flouting any rule she could. Jones claimed he had documented each instance, and he had told her he would fire her immediately if she committed another insubordinate act.

It took nearly a half hour to get the information out of Donna Dalrymple. Carolyn worked on the fact that Donna's presence was an admission of guilt. Finally Donna admitted that Jones had caught her with another student besides Bluefield.

When Donna finished, Carolyn called all of them back into the office and addressed them. "I'll help each of you as much as I can, but only if I get five resignations in my office first thing in the morning. Clarissa will get another chance, as I said. I'll check the legal aspects of all of this tonight. Most of you will probably be allowed to finish out the year, but that will be all."

She got only a few squawks of protest at this. Moments later they trudged dispiritedly out the door.

Meg, Carolyn, Scott, and I sat and stared at their empty chairs for a few minutes.

Finally Scott said, "We didn't get any closer to finding the murderer."

"I can't believe everything they told us," Carolyn said. "I feel almost obliged to tell the police. But it's going to be

169

bad enough for them to lose their jobs. Only one of them is a murderer."

"Maybe they were all in it together," Scott said.

"Could be," Meg said. "We can't discount it as a possibility, but the idea doesn't get us much closer to a solution."

"Which of them had anything to do with Marshall Longfellow?" I asked. "We've still got his murder as part of this."

"He saw something," Meg said. "That's the only thing that makes sense. He knew something and had to die. My guess is he saw someone and possibly could identify the killer."

"Maybe he didn't know he knew," I said.

We speculated on various possibilities for half an hour but got nowhere.

At one point I asked, "How come none of them noticed the other people's cars here in the parking lot and got suspicious?"

Carolyn said, "None of them were good friends. I doubt they'd know what kind of cars the others drove. We have three different lots. There's always cars in all of them much later than this for some activity or other."

We called it a night. Scott and I had left the car in the west parking lot. Meg and Carolyn were parked in the north lot. We parted at the front hall of the school. I needed to retrieve my briefcase from my classroom.

Scott and I walked down the corridors. He patted my shoulder and said, "Don't be discouraged. You had the right idea."

I shrugged. We walked mostly in darkness and shadows. Only the occasional exit sign lit the way. Five feet from my classroom, I said, "Hold it. Something's wrong. Something smells funny." It was an odd, out-of-place smell. In this wing of the school you get the smell of musty sweat, chalk, old wood, and an almost comfortable dankness.

A blob of greater darkness emerged from the recess of the door next to that of my room.

"Hold it right there," a harsh voice commanded.

A far light let me see the gleam of a gun; a moment later the side of the face caught the light. I recognized the senior Bluefield.

He jerked the gun at us. "In the room," he ordered.

I knew we were too far from any of the others in the building for them to hear and come to our rescue. The custodians usually cleaned this end of the building first. We wouldn't be disturbed.

Bluefield wore black jeans and a black sweatshirt. He'd tied his long blond hair in a ponytail.

"Sit in the chairs in the back," he ordered.

We sat. He kept the lights off. Dappled light streamed into the room through the unfallen leaves of the trees outside my classroom window. The lights and shadows swayed as the wind played among the foliage outdoors.

Bluefield shoved desks aside. Soon we sat at a two-desk island a few feet from the rear of the room. Even if someone passed in the hallway, they couldn't see us in the back. Bluefield paced in front of us. His right hand spasmed around the gun. He clenched and unclenched his left fist, his ragged and uneven breaths attesting to his heightened state of excitement. His eyes were narrowed, his pupils nearly invisible. All these were signs to me that we were in deep trouble. The man was out of control and would easily do murder.

For now he wanted to talk.

"You fuckers. Why the hell did you have to mess in my life? I had it good. A decent living. A house in the suburbs. Why the hell did you two faggots have to fuck it up? You couldn't mind your own business, so I'm going to have to mind yours for you." He gave us a nasty grin. "I planned this while they had me locked up. I've been watching the school. I never saw you come out today, so I decided to snoop around. I watched you from down the hall while you talked in the office." He pulled four pairs of handcuffs and placed them on the floor three feet in front of the desk where I sat.

He said, "Mason, you get the handcuffs." He moved to

the center of the room. "If you make any sudden moves, I will kill your boyfriend." He leveled the gun at Scott.

I carefully stretched for the handcuffs. When I had them, he instructed Scott to put his hands behind him. I shackled Scott's hands to the chair's bottom rungs, the shelf where the students put their books. Bluefield made me cuff my right arm, then moved closer to finish the job himself. He held the gun rigidly on Scott. He reminded me, "You make the slightest move, faggot, this gun goes off and your boyfriend dies."

When he finished the job, Bluefield sat in the lotus position in the middle of the floor. Light from outside gleamed off the left side of his face. His half-grin disappeared in darkness. He drew a deep breath and let out a deep sigh of satisfaction.

"I've been trying to get at you fags for days," he said.

"You burned the house down," I said.

"Yes. I wish you'd been in it. This will be better. I'll get to watch you die. I'll enjoy that. Harassing my kid was stupid, but I've planned to do this ever since you got in my way."

"Your son is going to have a miserable life," Scott said.

"Half the dumb-shit adults said that to me when I was a kid." He laughed loud and long. "It was a joke with me and my buddies. I'd only be rotten in a few classes each year. To the others I'd suck up and kiss ass. Used to drive teachers nuts. They'd argue about me, half the staff saying I was a saint. One old faggot who thought a cute thin blond kid would never do anything wrong was my biggest defender. The stupid fool. I hated him as much as the rest of them. Maybe I hated him the most. I could see him sneaking looks at my crotch in class." He laughed loud and long. "I was the class pusher and voted least likely to succeed. I bet I make more money than half of them."

Scott said, "Then at least we have the satisfaction of knowing we stopped you, took away your livelihood."

"I'll be back in business soon enough, and if not, I'll have the satisfaction of knowing you both are dead. So I win."

He stood up. Deliberately he hunted around the room for any kind of paper. He emptied the drawers of my desk into a pile in the middle of the doorway. On top of this he added the posters from the wall, then books from the shelves. It took him ten minutes because he had to keep his gun trained on us. While he collected material, he derided and sneered at us. But through all this I kept myself still. I didn't want him to notice the fatal flaws in his plan.

Bluefield examined his pile of trash with satisfaction. He added several of the wooden desks to the heap, then pulled a lighter out of his jeans pocket.

Scott said, "You can't believe you'll get away with this."

I wanted Scott to shut up. I didn't want Bluefield to think too much. One of the things I'd learned as the union building rep was never to underestimate the stupidity of human beings. It was Bluefield's stupidity, along with his out-of-control emotions, that I hoped would save us.

Bluefield said, "Why shouldn't I get away with this? I've got an alibi set up with some buddies. I'm out of this. Even when the fire alarm goes off and somebody gets here to save you, it'll be too late. They won't want to leap through the flames—if you're still alive when they get here."

He stepped around his pile halfway out the door. I could still see his face behind the debris. His eyes glowed in the flickering light. "Now, I don't want to see the two of you try to squirm or move while this gets going, otherwise I will simply shoot you. It'll be more fun this way, watching you burn to death. I wish I could do it more slowly." He swung the gun at us. "I'll blow huge holes in you if you try to move." He leaned down. Moments later flames leaped upward, from the trash, then quickly licked at the wooden doorframe.

Quickly the heat rose to that of a summer campfire. I felt sweat begin to bead on my skin. The smoke drifted out the doorway.

For a few more moments we listened to the sound of oxygen combining with the elements, then ear-piercing beeps began sounding all along the corridor. Even in the old section they'd installed smoke alarms.

The dimness helped us because Bluefield could no longer see our actions. I think the speed with which the fire grew surprised him, too. The heat and smoke drove him too far into the hall to effectively menace us with his gun.

Shots rang out. Wood splintered in the wall above our heads. A last desperate gasp by Bluefield as he turned to run, was my guess.

Two things wrong with Bluefield's plan: He couldn't see us because of his own fire, and he'd attached us to the old desks. While our hands were encumbered, our feet were free. He'd never come close enough for us to stand and attack him; with the desks still attached, it was too easy for him to dart away. But now we both simply stood up.

Fire blocked our way to the door. The flames caught the old wooden cabinets and inched up the walls. The warped and leaky windowpanes stood between us and clean air.

I could now hear fire trucks wailing in the distance, adding to the din of the fire alarms. Awkwardly, encumbered by the desk, I moved as rapidly as possible, as far toward the heat as I could. Then, with a desperate rush, I flung myself toward the back wall. The desk splintered on impact. Scott followed suit. Our arms still cuffed, we hurried to the window ledge, swung our bodies on top of it, and stood up. I felt sweat dripping from my forehead and heard Scott cough from the smoke. Desperate kicks splintered glass and wood. The rush of oxygen from outside fanned the flames, but we leaped through the opening.

As I flew out, I felt a stab into the side of my left leg. After we landed, I glanced down to see my pant leg ripped completely up the side and a jagged piece of glass embedded in my thigh and sticking out of it three inches. I gasped in pain. I looked for Scott. He lay on his side about three feet from me, gulping in bushels of fresh air.

I looked back at the school. Smoke and flame roared from my classroom. I felt hands pulling me back, looked up to see a fresh-faced fireman.

They got my leg to stop bleeding. We sipped cups of excellent coffee and watched the firemen. They confined the blaze to the one wing, but both floors went up. An hour after the fire started, the roof of the section fell in.

We'd told the first cops to show up about Bluefield; Daniels and Johnson arrived about five minutes after the roof collapsed. We told them they should examine the fire for spent shells and compare them to Bluefield's gun. I said they might catch him before he thought to pitch it, especially if he believed we were dead. They said they'd check it out.

Carolyn showed up. She offered her place for us to stay the night. Glancing at my watch, I found it was only a little after nine. I told her we needed to be in the city. I wanted the comfort of Scott's place.

We stopped at the hospital to get my cut leg stitched up. I saw the same doctor who had handled me a couple of days ago. He was young and attractive. He smiled winningly at me, but smiled even more brightly at—and spent an inordinate amount of time applying salve to what I thought were very minor cuts and bruises on the *non*pitching arm of—the winningest pitcher in baseball for the past ten years.

In the car Scott said, "The doctor was cute."

I said, "Sometimes your popularity is a pain in the ass."

He pulled onto I-80, merged with traffic, then said, "Sorry, I was just making conversation."

I let a mile or so pass, then apologized too. I went on: "I thought we really had something today, with my little plot. Nero Wolfe always pulls off the big confrontation-confession scene."

He put his hand on my thigh. "We gave it our best shot."

I sighed.

At the penthouse, on the couch in the living room. Lights in the apartment off, glow from the city providing enough light to see his white jockey shorts and the golden down on his chest. I put a Gordon Bok tape in the cassette player. Scott lay with his head in my lap. I leaned back and listened to Bok sing "Saben the Woodfitter." One of the quiet classics of folk music. I caressed Scott's chest hair with my fingertips, put my arm under his head, smelled his clean shower smell, sighed in near contentment.

The tape moved to the next song and Scott said, "I was a little scared for a while there tonight."

"Fortunately for us, Bluefield is not the brightest."

"I'm serious," he said. "I was scared."

I looked down. I could see the blue of his eyes searching mine. I traced his hairline, brushed a blond lock or two into place.

"I was too," I said.

We wound up on the living-room floor, on an Indian rug woven by one of his teammates.

I arrived at school early the next morning. The kids had been given the day off so the faculty and administration could get together to figure out how to hold classes.

The fire department met with us first, explaining which parts of the building they would let classes meet in.

While much of the vast complex remained intact, it would be necessary to run double shifts for the rest of the year. This meant that some teachers didn't start until eleven in the morning and wouldn't be going home until nearly five. No teacher I knew liked double shifts. We heard a lot of grumbling as they decided who would take what time period.

I saw all of our suspects at some time the next morning, whether in the front hall or the teachers' lounge; none of them acknowledged my existence. I felt distinctly unpopular.

I'd tried to call the police several times during the day, and at noon had gone out to talk to the people poking through the remains of the fire. They told me nothing, and a burly old fireman urged me vigorously to keep the hell out of their way. The police hadn't told me anything about the pursuit of Bluefield. He could be lurking nearby, with a dual attack with his son planned as his next move.

The doling out of the unburned books and materials

took up the majority of the afternoon. Saying that some teachers are pack rats is as ridiculous as saying the sun will rise. I've seen teachers who save a copy of every ditto, test, and homework assignment they've ever given. Some never throw anything out, in hopes that someday it may come in handy. Getting them to part with some of their precious materials took direct commands from heads of departments, and in one vicious dispute in the math department, Carolyn Blackburn had to step in. It was nearly six before I got out of the building. I spent the last hour helping referee a fight between the Senior Honors English teacher and Al Welman over who would get to use the remaining copies of *Great Expectations*.

I endured a ten-minute tirade from Al Welman. I wanted to whap the old fool over the head with his multihued umbrella, today's accessory of individualism.

Tired and discouraged, I strode out to my truck. I noted the glorious sunset and gorgeous colors and plodded on. I thought about northern Wisconsin and fall colors and hoped the leaves hadn't completely turned so far north.

I got within ten feet from my truck and stopped. A body detached itself from the driver's side. In size and shape it could have been Bluefield father or son.

I felt annoyance more than anything else. Maybe I could simply pound the shit out of him and be done with it. Then again, this could be the elder Bluefield and his gun.

I shifted my briefcase to my left hand, freeing my right in case I needed to defend myself, and checked for the possibility of ambush or for possible help from a passerby. Lots of places to hide in the parking lot, and no one around at the moment.

The body moved into the light, to reveal Dan.

He said, "Hello, Mr. Mason." He sounded respectful and calm.

The black paint of the truck gleamed in the last rays of the sun. I saw the two of us reflected in the surface.

"What can I do for you, Dan?" I asked.

He shuffled his feet, glanced up at me, then away.

"They arrested my dad an hour ago."

I grunted acknowledgment.

"I'm pretty fucked up sometimes," he said.

I remained silent and watchful.

He finally looked at me. The side of his face that caught the light looked troubled and unhappy. "It's like sometimes I can't control myself. Sometimes I feel like I'm going to bust. Not because I'm high, or angry, just like there's something inside of me that is bigger than me."

"Did you kill Mr. Jones?" I asked.

He looked startled, then gave me a brief smile. "No. I guess you're still in trouble because of that."

"I think I'm still a suspect."

"I didn't kill him. He was a fool, but he was friendly. A couple times I almost trusted him."

He scuffed his foot on the pavement, back and forth, for several minutes. Silence lengthened and more shadows gathered. I waited for whatever it was he came to say.

With his head still hanging down he whispered, "I hate my dad." His whole body seemed to shudder. He stuck his hands in his pockets.

I didn't know what to say, so I kept my mouth shut.

He said, "You really know Scott Carpenter? You guys are really boyfriends?"

"Yes."

He shook his head. "I wish I'd gotten his autograph."

We spent a few more minutes in silence. Only the glow of sunset remained touching the western horizon. To our east, darkness reigned.

"I'm sorry," Dan said. "For all the stuff I did."

I accepted his apology. We talked for a while, both leaning against the side of my truck. He made no promises about reform or change or what he wanted to do with the rest of his life. He did not break down sobbing in tears. He was a confused young adult doing a little talking.

As we spoke, the parking lot emptied of cars. A few of the faculty saw us. We got some strange looks. Meg waved but didn't come over to chat.

Dan said, "What's going to happen to my dad?"

"My best guess is he'll get charged with arson, probably attempted murder."

"He really hated you, Mr. Mason. You're the first person I've ever known that he didn't frighten or bully into giving him his way. That's part of the reason I'm here apologizing. I wish there was something I could do to help you out."

"Maybe there is," I said.

He leaned up a little straighter, looking wary.

"I'm not going to ask for secrets about drugs or illegal activity," I said. "I just want you to tell me everything you remember about the night of the murder. From the time you got back from the hospital until you left."

The sodium arc lights in the parking lot flicked to life, giving his blond hair a slightly reddish sheen.

Dan told his story. He'd come in with Jones. They'd talked for a few minutes. Jones had pressed him again to get psychiatric counseling. "I got mad at that. He was always bugging me about it."

Maybe Jones hadn't been as much of a milquetoast with the kid as I'd thought.

Dan had walked away. Georgette was still in the office when he walked out. Dan hunted for Dalrymple to talk to her, but at first he couldn't find her. He knew she usually didn't leave until late, so he hunted all over the school for her.

"Who did you see?"

"I found Donna, Mrs. Dalrymple. We talked a few minutes. I left her and walked out. Everybody was gone. I saw the janitor, the old guy who's in charge. He seemed all excited about something."

"How could you tell he was excited?"

"He kept singing to himself—something about 'I'm in the money.' I figured maybe he just won the lottery. The old fool practically danced down the hall with a cane."

"He was blackmailing the killer," I said. "Maybe he walked in on whoever did it."

We talked for a while longer, but Dan remembered nothing else significant about that night.

I wished him luck as he left, and I meant it. He might or might not turn his life around, but I wished him well.

I turned to my truck and clambered into the seat. Because of the oversized tires I had a panoramic view of the grounds around the school. My eye roved over the façade of the structure On the third floor, in the front of the new section, a light gleamed in a lone window. Third from the left on the top floor should have been the English department office. I started the car, wondering who was upstairs.

At the edge of the parking lot it hit me. I backed up, turned around, and parked. I entered the building through the doors near the gym. A basketball game organized by the Park District with men from the community rumbled over the wooden floor. I mounted the stairs through the all-too-familiar darkened halls.

I opened the door of the English office. Al Welman sat at his desk, scribbling on a piece of paper. At the sound of the opening door, he turned. I got a wintry smile.

"What's going on, Al?" I asked.

"Because of you I have to replan every one of my lessons for the next month."

"I didn't set the fire, Al."

"But you agreed with everybody else about the distribution of books. You're just making my job harder."

I sat on top of the desk next to the one he was working at. He rubbed bloodshot eyes and sighed tiredly.

He said, "On days like this, I used to be able to go home and Mabel would have dinner ready and hot tea on the stove." He sighed. "I miss her."

I said, "It's Wednesday, Al. Where's your cane? You bring the umbrella on Fridays."

He put his red pen down.

"I talked to a witness who saw the blackmailer with a cane just after the murder."

Al's right hand shook nearly uncontrollably as he tried to lift his cup of tea to his lips.

"My cane's at home," he croaked.

I said, "Let's go look."

He shook his head.

"I thought you and Marshall were friends," I said.

The tea spilled on a pile of student papers on the desk. He mopped at it clumsily.

"Marshall found the cane at the scene," I said. "He was going to blackmail you. Why would a close friend turn on you?"

Welman sighed, then told the story. "Marshall needed money. He wanted out of this place. He knew he was going to get fired soon. He saw this as a way to get a free meal ticket for the rest of his life. I had to shut him up."

I listened to his confession, his plotting and planning, the theft of the knife, waiting for the right moment in Jones's office when no one was around. In his excitement he'd dropped his cane, gone back for it, but it was gone. Then Marshall had begun the blackmail. They were to meet last Sunday. Welman found him asleep on the roof and took the chance to smother him. He'd tried to get into Longfellow's home since then to try and recover the cane, but he'd been unsuccessful. After a while he figured that even if the police found the cane in Longfellow's house, they'd never associate it with him. Only someone from the school could do that.

I called the police from the phone in the office. As we waited for them to arrive, Al said, "Jones was a mean man. If he'd been a little understanding, a little nicer, I could have retired in a couple years in peace." His last words to me just before the police walked in were "I'm glad I killed him."

On the shores of Lake Superior we huddled in our fur lined black-leather jackets against a rising north wind. A cloudless sky glowed faintly blue in the west as we watched shadows grow around us. We stood on a rocky promontory on one of the last reaches of an island that was still technically a part of Wisconsin. From our vantage point we could barely see the twinkle of light from the windows of our cabin. No other sign of human habitation disturbed the serenity of the moment. Scott put his arm around me and we moved close.